Poisoning at the Party

NIGHTMARE ARIZONA
PARANORMAL COZY MYSTERIES

BETH DOLGNER

Poisoning at the Party
Nightmare, Arizona Paranormal Cozy Mysteries, Book Five
© 2024 Beth Dolgner

Print ISBN: 978-1-958587-16-4

Poisoning at the Party is a work of fiction. Names, characters, places, and incidents either are the products of the author's imagination or are used fictitiously. Any resemblance to actual persons, living or dead, businesses, companies, events, or locales is entirely coincidental.

Published by Redglare Press
Cover by Dark Mojo Designs
Print Formatting by The Madd Formatter

https://bethdolgner.com

CHAPTER ONE

The seatbelt tightened against my chest as Mama braked hard, her vintage red Mustang sliding just a bit along the dirt road before coming to an abrupt stop. A cloud of dust swirled around us.

Beside me, Mama let out a shaky breath. She was staring ahead at the crest of the low hill that separated us from Nightmare Sanctuary Haunted House.

"Mama, what's wrong?" I asked, turning slightly in the passenger seat and putting a hand on her arm.

Mama shook her head, her gray fluffy waves shifting with the motion. "I haven't been here since we gave up looking for my sister. I've ignored everyone who lives and works at the Sanctuary for the past forty years, Olivia. Will they even want to see me after I abandoned them?"

I squeezed Mama's arm. "You didn't abandon them. Baxter asked you to take a step back from the supernatural world to protect Damien."

"Baxter didn't want Damien to know I'm his aunt," Mama corrected. She had such a tight grip on the steering wheel that I wondered if I would have to pry her fingers off, one by one, once we finally got to the Sanctuary. Unless, of course, she decided she couldn't go through with it and backed her Mustang down the narrow dirt road, all the way to the old gallows at the crossroads. "I could have kept up my friendships with the people here, while still keeping my promise to Baxter."

"That would have been difficult," I countered. "You would have still seen Baxter and Damien in passing, and it would have simply reminded Baxter and everyone else that you're his sister-in-law. Everyone at the Sanctuary adores Baxter, and they'll understand why you were willing to give up your connection to him and this place."

Mama's fingers relaxed slightly, and the car began to move forward slowly. When we reached the crest of the hill, Mama stopped again, but it was a much less violent experience the second time around. "Look at it," she said breathily. She leaned forward and rested her chin on the top of the steering wheel.

Baxter Shackleford had been smart to open his year-round haunted house attraction in the old building that lay before us. Originally home to the Nightmare Sanctuary Hospital and Asylum, the looming stone building was gray and weather stained. The circular driveway in front of the recessed double front doors was cracked and overgrown, and the grounds were choked with weeds that went right up to the foundation of the building.

It was an incredibly spooky-looking place.

I had been working at the Sanctuary for more than two months, so the facade had ceased to give me goosebumps. Mama, on the other hand, hadn't glimpsed it since the search for her missing sister, Lucille, had been abandoned more than forty years before.

And then Mama had abandoned her friends at the Sanctuary, at least in her mind.

"Damien's inside there, and he's not resentful toward you," I pointed out. "And you'll love Vivian. She's so sweet."

"She wasn't here back then. She has no reason to dislike me." Mama sighed. "You're right. There are old relationships to renew and repair, and new friends to make. I can't let my fear of rejection stop me."

"That's the spirit!"

Mama chuckled as she pressed the gas pedal again. "You showing up in this town really started an avalanche, you know."

"An avalanche in the middle of the desert?"

"Yes. It's no more strange than the fact there are vampires sleeping inside that building right now."

Mama had a point. She continued to look nervous, even after we parked and got out of her Mustang, and I knew it had nothing to do with the vampires. As we began our walk toward the front doors, I racked my brain to think of something comforting to say. Before I could come up with anything though, I heard someone shout, "Sue!"

I looked ahead to see two men coming toward us. One of them was Damien Shackleford, but he wasn't the one who had shouted Mama's name. Instead, it was Malcolm. I hadn't even realized he knew Mama.

Malcolm's long, lean legs had a big stride, and he closed the distance between us quickly. I knew his broad smile was genuine, even though it looked slightly sinister in his gaunt face. It only made him look more like a walking, talking skeleton.

Malcolm reached out and pulled Mama into a bear hug. She looked stiff at first, but then she relaxed and squeezed Malcolm tightly. "Still skin and bones, I see," she commented, looking up at him with a mischievous smile.

"I don't even diet," Malcolm said candidly. He stepped back and turned to walk next to us. Damien had reached us, too, but he simply said hello. I couldn't blame him: he had only found out Mama was his aunt a couple weeks before, so I was sure he was still getting used to the idea. He wasn't ready for big hugs just yet.

"Lucille was such a friend to me," Malcolm said to

Mama. "I always enjoyed your company, too. I understood Baxter's desire for secrecy, but I've missed our late-night talks."

Damien stopped walking. "You knew? All this time, you knew Mama was my aunt?"

Malcolm didn't look at all apologetic as he said, "Of course. You have to understand, Damien, that Baxter was afraid of what sort of supernatural abilities you might have inherited from Lucille. He didn't want you asking questions about your mother, or what she was capable of, and your father thought it was best to cut ties with Lucille's family."

Damien grumbled something under his breath, and the only part of it I caught was, "...said the same thing." Mama's explanation had been very similar to Malcolm's.

"Is everything set up for us?" I asked, anxious to change the subject.

"Yes," Damien answered. "Vivian has been napping all afternoon, so she'll have plenty of energy for the séance."

We had reached the front doors, and Damien moved ahead to open one of them for us. He was wearing a black three-piece suit, looking like he was going to a funeral or a fancy party rather than a séance where we would, hopefully, communicate with the spirit of his mother.

Damien was also wearing his mirrored sunglasses, which meant his emotions were probably heightened, and he didn't want anyone to see the telltale sign of his green eyes glowing.

I tried to give Damien a sympathetic look as I followed Mama through the door, but I was pretty sure he was glaring underneath his sunglasses.

We paused in the grand entryway as Mama slowly turned a full circle. "It looks mostly how I remember it." She pointed at the brass stanchions and red velvet ropes that were set up in the wide space, waiting for the tourists who would be lining up to go through the haunt that night. "Those are new, though."

Mama's gaze drifted to the wide stone staircase leading up to the old hospital rooms, which had been converted into sweet little apartments for many of the supernatural creatures who worked at the Sanctuary. Her nervous look had dissolved in the wake of Malcolm's warm welcome, but it returned, and I was sure she was thinking about all the people who were up there and wondering if they would be as understanding as Malcolm.

"This way," Damien called. Instead of going upstairs, we were going down. Damien led us to the basement, which I had only been in a couple times before. I knew the vampires—Mori and Theo—had their windowless apartments down there, and there were guest rooms for visiting vampires, but I didn't know there was much else to find in the basement except dusty old props for the haunted house.

We turned left down a hallway at the bottom of the basement stairs, and Damien stopped and knocked on the first door we reached.

"Come in!" called a feminine voice from inside.

Even as Damien reached for the door handle, the door opened, and we saw Vivian's husband, Amos, framed in the doorway. While Vivian was petite, Amos was big and broad. He waved a muscular arm. "We're ready!"

I introduced Mama to Amos, then turned to see Vivian sitting at a circular table covered in a burgundy cloth. There were wooden folding chairs positioned around the table, and a light fixture above emitted a soft golden glow from a frosted glass globe. There was one cabinet against the wall, but the rest of the room was bare, and the corners were filled with shadows.

Vivian stood and walked over to Mama, her hand extended. Her long dark hair was pulled up in a green bandana that paired beautifully with her cropped jeans and green cardigan. As Mama shook Vivian's hand, she thanked her for facilitating the séance.

"We all want to find Baxter and bring him home safely," Vivian said earnestly. "If we can get some answers about Lucille, too, then it might help us in the search for Baxter. It's all tied together."

Vivian motioned for us to sit around the table, and I wound up between Damien and Mama. So, when Vivian told all of us to take hands to form a circle, I could feel the way my cheeks warmed. I slid my hand into Damien's, wondering where I stood with him.

For that matter, I wondered where he stood with me. He had started to open up to me, and I no longer thought he was the biggest jerk in the world, but every time I felt like we were making progress in our friendship, he would close himself off again. I didn't like the back and forth. It was confusing.

And, sitting there holding hands with him, it was also really awkward.

"Now," Vivian said, "I want all of you to focus on Lucille. Damien, you have memories of your mother, even if they're from when you were a baby. They're in your mind, still, and you can call them forward if you concentrate. Olivia, I understand you've seen her picture. Sue—"

"Everyone calls me Mama, honey."

Vivian smiled. "Mama and Malcolm, you two should focus on your memories of Lucille."

After a few moments of silence, during which I focused on the green eyes and soft smile I remembered from an old photo of Lucille, Vivian lifted her chin and spoke toward the light fixture. "Lucille Shackleford, I am here with your son and your sister. Their friends have come, too. We ask that you please come sit with us. We wish to communicate with you, in whatever manner you prefer. I understand you were a psychic medium, like me, so you already know the tools available to you for communication. Please, Lucille, join us."

I felt a shiver work its way up my spine as the room began to grow cold. Beside me, I heard Damien suck in his breath, and I knew the chill wasn't my imagination.

The light began to pulse slowly, then it went out completely, plunging the room into complete darkness.

We all must have been holding our breath, because I couldn't hear anything. As I sat there in the dark and silence, I began to see a soft glow. It became brighter as it moved toward the table.

Then, I realized it wasn't one glowing object, but two. The ghosts of Butch Tanner and Connor McCrory, the outlaw and the sheriff who had killed each other in a shootout during Nightmare's Wild West days, had arrived.

Tanner and McCrory floated to Vivian's side, and in the ghostly glow they emanated, I could see Vivian's frown. "I wasn't trying to summon you two."

"Begging your pardon, ma'am," McCrory said, lifting his black cowboy hat as he nodded politely at Vivian. "We know you're looking for Missus Shackleford. She asked us to come speak to you on her behalf."

CHAPTER TWO

"Wait a minute," I said. I used the unexpected arrival of Tanner and McCrory to pull my hand out of Damien's grasp, and I pointed at the two ghosts. "Have you two been in contact with Lucille this whole time?"

"No," Tanner drawled behind the red bandana he wore over his mouth and nose. "We were upstairs with the witches, watching an old Western, when both of us heard a woman's voice telling us to come down here to pass along a message."

"Did the witches hear Lucille's voice, too?" Vivian asked. She had looked annoyed when Tanner and McCrory had first shown up, but now, she looked curious.

"They didn't hear a thing," Tanner said.

"Why won't Lucille come talk to me herself?" Vivian glanced toward the ceiling, like she was imagining the spirit of Lucille upstairs, watching TV in the apartment shared by Maida, Madge, and Morgan.

"You've heard what a gifted psychic she was," Mama said. "Chances are, she was worried she might overwhelm you. If she tried to channel through you, it could exhaust you, or worse."

Vivian's eyes widened as she turned to look at Mama. "Was she really that powerful?"

"As far as we know, Lucille didn't die. She simply made

the decision to cease existing in corporeal form. We think she did it because she was worried she might be too powerful—too dangerous—otherwise."

Vivian brought her hands up to the sides of her head. "Olivia has told me that theory before, but it's hard to wrap my brain around it."

"What," Damien said tensely, "is the message from my mother?"

"Oh, right, I was just coming to that," said McCrory. He straightened the lapels of his black duster and squared his shoulders, clearly proud to be passing on a spectral message. "She wanted us to say this: 'Train my son. Train the stranger.'"

Damien leaned toward McCrory. "And?"

"That's it."

"I need more than that!" Damien was nearly shouting. He had taken off his sunglasses before the séance began, and a quick glance showed that his eyes were glowing bright green in the dark room. "I want to speak to my mother!"

"She's not here," Vivian murmured. "I would feel her if she was."

Damien stood quickly, the chair clattering so loudly I knew it had toppled over backward. Once he turned his back on the table, I couldn't see his eyes anymore, but I could hear his footsteps. Then, there was a blindingly bright flash of light as he opened the door leading to the hallway, where the overhead lights were still on. The door slammed, and the room fell into silence and darkness again.

"And they always said I had bad manners," Tanner said with a sniff.

I stood to follow, but Mama, whose hand was still in mine, held me back. "Let him have some time," she said. Her voice was shaking.

"You're right, Mama," I said as I sat back down.

"Mama?" McCrory floated through the middle of the table until he was face-to-face with Mama. I would have laughed if I wasn't feeling shaken by Damien's dramatic exit. It looked funny to see the ghost's torso sticking out of the tablecloth. "Is that you, Missus Dalton?"

"Yeah. It's good to see you again, Connor."

McCrory let out a whoop of delight. "I didn't think I'd ever see you again! Welcome back, ma'am! You still married, or are you looking to go on a date with a man who's a little older than you?" McCrory raised one eyebrow suggestively.

This time, I did laugh. Watching a ghost flirt with Mama was too much, even though she replied with a smooth, "Benny is still among the living, so I'm not looking for love from the dead just yet."

The light overhead flickered back on, and I could see that Malcolm was suppressing his own laughter.

"Sorry about the theatrics," Tanner said. "We thought it would be fun to make a big entrance."

I rubbed my arms. "Next time, maybe don't make it so cold, okay?"

"Whatever you say, Miss Olivia."

Tanner and McCrory disappeared a few seconds later, presumably heading back upstairs to continue watching the Western along with the witches.

Vivian apologized for not being able to make direct contact with Lucille, but Mama waved it off. "That's not your fault. Clearly, Lucille didn't want to show up. She always was a headstrong girl."

We all thanked Vivian for conducting the séance, then we headed upstairs. Malcolm continued up to the second level while I walked Mama toward the front doors.

"Hang on a second," I told her just as she reached out and grasped one of the door handles. I sprinted down the hall to our left, which was where Damien's office was. The door was closed, and there was no answer to my knocking. I even tried opening the door, but it was locked.

I returned to Mama and admitted I had hoped to find Damien. When we reached the parking lot, though, his silver Corvette was nowhere to be seen. "I bet he went to the mine for some solitude," I said.

"Then I'll stop by there on my way back to the motel. He's had a little time to cool off, so maybe he'll be ready to talk."

I impulsively gave Mama a hug. "I know this was hard for you today, but thank you for coming. And good luck with Damien."

"From everything you've said about him, I'll need it." Mama gave me a little smile, then climbed into her car. I stood and watched until she had driven over the crest on the dirt road and disappeared from sight. She was heading to the mine, then back to her job at Cowboy's Corral Motor Lodge, and I was staying at the Sanctuary to do my job there.

By the time the nightly family meeting began, I had changed into my black Nightmare Sanctuary T-shirt and made three laps around the outside of the building in an effort to calm my nerves. All it really accomplished was prompting Zach, the werewolf who handled ticket sales, to ask me if I was training for the slowest marathon ever.

The meetings were held in the dining room, where long rows of tables and benches were set up in front of a podium on one end. The nights were getting longer, and by the time the meeting started, it was already completely dark outside the massive windows that looked out over the wild land behind the building.

I didn't hear at least half of what Justine, who managed the day-to-day operations of the Sanctuary, said to us during the family meeting. I was too busy worrying about Damien. The first half of Lucille's message, *train my son*, was pretty straightforward: she wanted Damien to explore his own supernatural abilities. That was in direct contrast to what his father had wanted. Baxter had taught Damien to suppress his abilities as soon as he had started exhibiting signs of them as a teenager.

Even if it was a direct order from his own mother, would Damien go against Baxter's wishes? And, more importantly, would he go against his own instincts? Damien was scared of what he might be capable of. He had never said it outright to me, but I knew it was true.

There was movement next to me, and I looked over to see that Mori's pet chupacabra, Felipe, had climbed onto the bench. He curled up beside me and rested his head in my lap. I stroked his gray leathery skin, and his tongue lolled out of his mouth.

"Thanks, Felipe," I whispered to him. "You must know that I need some cuddles from my favorite cryptid, but you're drooling on me." Little drops of drool were accumulating on the tips of his sharp fangs and falling onto my jeans.

"Now," Justine began loudly, and I finally started paying attention, "the Nightmare Fall Festival begins this weekend, which means the annual kickoff party for it happens on Thursday night."

There were a few groans from the Sanctuary employees seated around me.

"I know, I know," Justine said, raising her hands defensively. "But we've been working with the festival for the past twelve years. They let us have a promotional booth there for free, in exchange for us doing a little haunting at their kickoff party. I know it stretches us thin to do that on top of dealing with the October crowds here at the Sanctuary, but we have our temp staff with us to make sure everything is covered."

I scanned the crowd and realized that yes, in fact, there were about six faces I hadn't seen before. If I hadn't been so distracted, I probably would have noticed earlier.

"Several of the temps will be at the fall festival party on Thursday, as well as a few of you regulars," Justine continued. "After that, the temps will both man our booth at the festival and help out around here. Tonight, I'm going to have them team up with some of you so they can learn the ropes."

Justine began going down a list, pairing the newcomers with longtime employees. I hadn't expected to be included. After all, I had only worked at the Sanctuary for a couple of months. People like Malcolm and Theo had been there for decades. So, when Justine said my name, I jumped in surprise. Felipe lifted his head from my lap and looked up at me with narrowed eyes.

Great, now I've annoyed the chupacabra.

Justine had assigned me to my usual role of taking tickets at the front, and I was going to be paired with a temp employee named Daniel. Since I'd just roused Felipe, I was sliding him off my lap when a man who looked like he was around thirty sat down across from me. "Hi, you're Olivia, right?"

"I am. You must be Daniel."

Daniel smiled as he tossed his long, lank brown hair out of his face. "You weren't here last year."

"I'm new, but it sounds like you're not. Did you work the front doors last year?"

"Nope. They had me out at the festival during the weekends, and on weekdays, I played a zombie in the hospital scene here at the haunt. It was so fun, and totally worth the trip down from Utah."

"You came all the way from Utah for this gig?"

"The temp staff comes from all over the Southwest. Not just anyone can work at this place." Daniel gave me a lazy salute. "Now, lead on! I'm ready to be trained in the ways of ticket taking!"

"You'll be a pro in the first ten minutes," I said, rising. "It's the questions you have to be ready for. You'll be giving a lot of people directions to the bathrooms and assuring the scaredy-cats that they'll be just fine." I smiled to myself as I led Daniel out of the dining room and in the direction of the entryway. On my first night at the Sanctuary, Zach had given me a primer on what questions visitors most frequently asked, and now, I was getting to pass along that same info.

I was more of an old-timer at the Sanctuary than I had realized.

As we walked into the entryway, I noticed several of the stanchions had been shoved together, probably to clean the floor or to make way for someone carrying something big through the room. "We'll need to put those back in place before we let folks inside," I said.

Daniel lifted an arm, his long fingers stretched toward the stanchions. "I'll do it."

As I watched, the stanchions flew apart from each other, one of them tipping over and landing with a clatter on the stone floor.

CHAPTER THREE

"I'm not the best at controlling it," Daniel said with a shrug. He gave me a lopsided grin.

"Telekinesis," I guessed, looking from Daniel to the stanchions.

"Yeah. Some of our kind are very precise. My style is a little more chaotic." Daniel loped forward and picked up the fallen stanchion. "Are these at least close to where they should be now?"

"Closer, at any rate. Your chaos saved us a bit of work."

Together, we moved the stanchions into their rightful spots. I was still getting used to Justine's brand of telekinesis, which was smooth and often subtle. Daniel, on the other hand, seemed to take more of a "bull in a china shop" approach to his supernatural ability. Justine had once slid a mug of beer across a table to me. I hated to imagine what it would look like if Daniel tried to do that.

Before long, we had opened one of the front doors, and Daniel was taking tickets and welcoming guests. Since it was a Tuesday, the crowds weren't overwhelming, but business was steady. As we approached Halloween, each night's crowds seemed bigger than the last.

During a brief lull in welcoming visitors, Daniel said

casually, "You're lucky you were paired with me, you know."

I couldn't tell if Daniel was joking, or if he was just really vain. "Oh?" I said.

"Yeah. If you had been paired with Annabelle, you'd be doing all the work yourself."

"She's another one of the temp employees," I guessed.

Daniel paused to take a pair of tickets, then turned to me. "She was here last Halloween, too. She's useless. That guy Baxter ran a tight ship. If he was still here, I doubt he would have hired her again. Is it true Baxter just disappeared?"

"Yeah, almost eight months ago now. We haven't been able to get a lead on what happened to him."

"Too bad. He would have made smarter hiring decisions."

I was tempted to protest that Justine and Damien both made perfectly fine decisions when it came to running the Sanctuary, but I stopped myself. For one thing, I certainly hadn't agreed with Damien's management style when he had arrived in Nightmare to take over his father's business. Plus, I doubted Daniel would much care what I thought about it.

"Of course, that guy running the fall festival makes pretty bad hiring decisions, too," Daniel continued. "He had talked to me about working part-time out there during the day, before my Sanctuary shift each night. I really needed the money because I was behind on my rent and my roommates were threatening to kick me out, but then he went and gave the job to Annabelle, instead."

"That's too bad you didn't get the extra money. Were you able to work things out with your roommates?"

"No. They kicked me out. But I eventually landed in a good place, so no hard feelings, right?" Daniel looked like he did, in fact, have some very hard feelings.

We had a flood of people after that, so it was a while before we spoke again. I was about to ask Daniel what he did for a living during the rest of the year, but he started the conversation with, "Last year, Annabelle was supposed to be in the cemetery scene, but she just wandered off. That creepy banshee lady found her outside, flirting with some guy."

This time, I did speak up in defense of my friends. "Fiona isn't creepy." I mean, sure, she was a banshee and a harbinger of death, but that wasn't her fault. She was a kind, intelligent person whom I was happy to call a friend.

The night passed swiftly, thanks to the stream of people pouring through the doors, but by the end of it, I couldn't tell how I felt about Daniel. He was a good worker, for sure, and he was great with the guests, but his griping about his fellow temp Annabelle left a sour taste in my mouth.

After we closed at midnight, I congratulated Daniel on a job well done, then made a beeline for the staff bathroom so I could retrieve my purse from my locker there. Before I could go in, though, I heard someone behind me calling my name.

I knew it was Clara before I even turned around. She had a high, childlike voice that fit perfectly with her thin face and pointed fairy ears.

"Hey, Clara," I said brightly, even as I realized she had a worried expression on her face. "Oh, no, what's wrong?"

"Nothing. But I heard about what happened at the séance earlier. I figured you were planning to go find Damien, but you don't need his drama tonight. You're going out instead!"

I laughed. "Actually, I was planning to go home and sleep, but I'm happy to go out. Are we heading to Under the Undertaker's?"

"Of course. Justine is coming, too, and we'll drive over together in twenty minutes."

"I'll be ready," I promised. I popped into the locker room and changed back into the blue blouse I had arrived in. Paired with my black jeans and sneakers, it wasn't exactly a "going out" look, but Under the Undertaker's was a fairly casual place. If our resident gargoyle, Gunnar, could go there with no clothes on, then I would be fine in my jeans.

Clara had implied we were going out to keep me from chasing after Damien, but the second Justine joined me under the portico at the Sanctuary's entrance, I knew we were going for her. She had a frazzled look, and she clearly needed to unwind.

I reached out and pulled a bit of moss out of Justine's long chestnut waves. Usually, her hair looked spectacular, but at the moment, it looked like she had gotten into a brawl with an alley cat.

"Ugh." Justine eyed the moss between my fingers with distaste. "One of the prop trees in the witches' vignette dropped a big branch tonight. It apparently missed a guest by only a few inches. I had to help with cleanup since it was blocking the pathway."

"Rough night, then?"

"We also had a guest faint in the middle of the cemetery, then someone tried to go through one of the staff doors to the tunnels. And then a few of the temps—"

"Girl, save it for the bar!" Clara had just come out of the building, and she raised a finger like she was lecturing Justine. "The stories will seem less stressful if you tell them over a cocktail."

Justine sighed deeply. "You're right. Let's go."

Soon, the three of us were at the door of Under the Undertaker's. The entrance to the bar for supernatural creatures was off an alley that ran behind High Noon Boulevard, where tourists flocked to soak up the Wild West architecture and atmosphere. They bought souvenirs and watched reenactment gunfights all day long, without ever guessing there was a secret bar below the coffee shop that served up overpriced lattes.

Now that the weather had cooled down after the oppressive summer heat, the dumpsters in the alley didn't smell nearly as bad as we made our way past them to the bar's entrance. Clara knocked on the nondescript door, and a small window in it slid open. A pair of violet eyes stared out, looking much like Clara's own.

"Hey, Aunt April," Clara said.

Aunt April's eyes darted toward me, then Justine. Then, the window slid shut with a metallic clang, and the door opened. We went inside and down the spiral staircase that led into the basement-level bar.

Since it was a Tuesday, the bar wasn't that busy. There were plenty of unoccupied chairs around the low tables. Candlelight flickered against the long curtains hung from the ceiling, which helped provide a cozy atmosphere and set the tables apart just enough to offer a bit of privacy.

A few of the temps who were helping out at the Sanctuary for the remainder of October were sitting at one table. Justine smiled and waved at them before giving Clara a meaningful look. Clara seemed to take the hint, guiding us to a table as far from the temps as possible.

"Was the person who fainted okay?" I asked Justine, picking up on our conversation from before.

"Not until we have drinks in front of us!" Clara reminded me.

"He was fine," Justine said with a casual wave of her hand. "Something about blood sugar and having not eaten dinner before coming to the Sanctuary. Honestly, though, I think he just got scared and didn't want to admit it in front of his friends."

"You said it was in the cemetery vignette," I pointed out, "and if Fiona was wailing up a storm, I can see how someone might get a little lightheaded."

A woman who looked nearly two decades younger than me came up to our table, a tray full of drinks balanced on the palm of one hand. Her silvery hair seemed to shimmer in the candlelight. "Clara, Justine, the usual?"

Both women nodded.

"And you?" the server asked, looking at me.

"Gin and tonic, please," I said.

"Coming right up." The server bustled off, heading for the table full of temps.

We continued our conversation, until Clara sat up straight and looked around the bar. "We should have had our drinks by now."

"Yeah," Justine agreed. "It's not like the place is busy."

Right at that moment, our server appeared with three drinks on her tray. Her face had looked bright and friendly earlier, but this time, she was scowling. She slammed the glasses down on the table so hard that some of my drink sloshed over the rim. "Here," she growled.

"Callie, what's going on? Is this about me borrowing your sweater without asking?" Clara asked.

"No." Callie ground out the word, and her head turned in the direction of the temps.

"Did one of them say something rude to you?" Justine half-rose from her chair, looking ready to give someone what for.

"No."

Clara glanced at me. "This is my little sister, Callie. Usually, she's more talkative."

That got Callie to look down at us again, but I really

wished she hadn't. Her eyes were a darker shade of violet than Clara's, and she looked so mad I almost expected sparks to fly out of them.

"She's back," Callie spat. "That selfish, heartless fairy who ruined my life. I hope she drops dead."

CHAPTER FOUR

Justine, Clara, and I all turned as one to stare at the temps. "Who do you mean?" I asked.

Callie shrugged. "Oh, she's not here. She knows better. But I heard them talking about her when I was delivering the drinks. They're so excited she's back. Pushovers."

"You know, Olivia here has a bad habit of winding up in the middle of murder investigations," Clara said in a teasing tone. "You should be careful about wishing death on someone when she's in earshot."

"I'm not going to murder anyone." Callie sounded deflated. "I mean, I know I just said I hope she drops dead, but I'm not planning to make it happen. I'm just hoping for, I don't know, a freak lightning storm or something."

Clara stood and put an arm around her sister's shoulders. "I'm teasing you, but I also know how much she hurt you. I saw her earlier, but I didn't have the heart to break the news to you that she's back."

Justine was looking between the two fairies, and she finally said, "Callie, did one of my temps do something to you?"

"You don't know the story?" Clara asked, surprised.

Justine shook her head.

"To be fair, it happened three years ago in a completely

different city," Callie said. She leaned her head on Clara's shoulder.

"Callie had a great boyfriend while she was going to school in Phoenix," Clara explained. "He left her for another fairy named Annabelle. She showed up at the Sanctuary last year to work the Halloween season, and we made sure to keep her away from here."

"Annabelle?" I said, surprised. "The temp teamed up with me tonight complained about her nonstop. He said she was useless."

"She's also heartless. I thought when I left Phoenix, I'd never have to see her again." Callie lifted her head and sighed. "I had asked Baxter to please not hire her back."

Justine pressed a hand to her forehead. "Oh, Callie, I'm so sorry. Baxter didn't leave any notes about the temps from last year, and with him missing, he couldn't pass on the request. I just hired the same crew again, because I didn't know."

"And I didn't think to say anything," Clara said.

"It's not your fault, Justine. Or yours, Sis." Callie looked around at the three of us. "Make sure she doesn't show up here, okay? And I'll steer clear of the Sanctuary and the Nightmare Fall Festival, like I did last year."

We all promised to keep the two of them from running into each other. As Callie walked away, I heard her mutter, "I used to *love* Halloween."

It was hard to feel any sense of relaxation after that exchange. Justine felt terrible for inadvertently hiring someone who had hurt Callie, and Clara was bemoaning the fact she hadn't thought to tell Justine about the situation. Justine didn't even fill us in on the other stressful incidents that had prompted our visit to Under the Undertaker's in the first place, and I expected it was because she didn't want to drag the mood down even further.

I walked home after we finished our drinks, feeling worried. I was concerned about Damien and anxious to see him after his reaction to the séance earlier. At the same time, I felt a strong sense of obligation to uphold my promise to Callie, and I pictured myself on fairy security duty until the end of October. I hadn't even met Annabelle yet, and already, she was causing me problems.

When I woke up on Wednesday morning, I showered and dressed quickly, then poured my coffee and took it with me to the front office of Cowboy's Corral Motor Lodge. My apartment was at the back corner of the motel, but it was a short walk to the front of the property, where the two-story cinder-block building that housed the office and lobby sat.

I found Mama standing behind the counter, checking out a family with two kids. She gave me a little wink when I walked in, and I hoped that meant she had good news to share about Damien.

The bell on the glass door of the office was still tinkling in the wake of the family's exit when I asked, "Was he at the mine last night?"

"He was, and I think it's good we gave him a little time to cool off before trying to reason with him."

I frowned. "How much of a jerk was he to you?"

"He wasn't a jerk at all," Mama said quickly. Since he had returned to Nightmare, Mama had been keen to paint Damien in a positive light. Of course, at the time, I hadn't known it was because she was secretly his aunt. "He's struggling, though. This is the closest he's gotten to having a mother since he was small, and she wants him to explore the power his father taught him to be afraid of. He's torn between which path to choose, and he's scared."

"He said all that to you?" I asked, amazed. For someone who didn't like to open up, it sounded like Damien had really poured his heart out to Mama.

"Oh, no, of course not," Mama said with an incredulous laugh. "I learned a lot more from his body language and the tone of his voice than I did from anything he said. He's going to need your support, Olivia."

"I'm trying, but he's not exactly an open book."

"That doesn't matter. Even if he doesn't confide in you about what he's feeling, he still needs to know that you've got his back. Besides, he'll open up in time."

I traced the rim of my coffee mug with a finger as I thought back over the times Damien had started to warm up to me, then clammed up again. "You're right. He's making progress, but he seems to take two steps forward and one step back."

Mama winked at me again. "Sounds like he needs to take you dancing."

I rolled my eyes, but I couldn't help snickering at Mama's joke. "I meant metaphorical steps."

"You know Lucille's message yesterday was about you, too." The mirth had disappeared from Mama's face, and she looked at me gravely.

"You mean the line about training the stranger," I said, nodding. "I thought maybe it was about me. You told me that the night before I arrived in Nightmare, you had a dream in which you heard Lucille's voice telling you to welcome the stranger."

"I don't know how she knew you were coming, but she did. And, I think, she already knew you were a conjuror, even though you didn't. She sensed your potential even though you were miles away."

I had told Mama how convinced Damien was that I was something called a conjuror, a person who could wish for something so hard they actually made it happen. I had also admitted to Mama that I finally believed it. What had eventually convinced me was hearing Baxter's disembodied voice inside the mine he had turned into a home—and something of a paranormal prison—for himself and Lucille.

"I've been trying to get Damien to explore his powers, but maybe hearing it from his mother will finally get him to do it," I said. "I'm going to leave for work early tonight so I can talk to him. Hopefully, he'll be willing to set aside some time to start finding out what he's capable of."

"Be patient with him."

"I will be," I promised Mama.

True to my word, I arrived at the Sanctuary thirty minutes before the family meeting. There were already cars in the parking lot, and I knew we were in for another busy night, even though it was the middle of the week.

Damien's office door was open, and he looked up as I walked in. "I figured you'd show up to check on me," he said. His tone was too neutral for me to know if that made him happy, or if he was annoyed by me actually caring about his well-being.

"Of course. I—"

"No."

I cocked my head in confusion. "No, what?"

"You've asked me before if I want to start exploring my abilities. I said no then, and that's still my answer."

"But, Damien, even your mother—"

"No."

"If we're ever going to find—"

Damien stood up abruptly, his eyes flashing. Before he could say no a third time, I held up my hands and took a step back. "Okay," I said quickly. "Sorry."

Damien's anger and his intense stare made me feel so uncomfortable I didn't know what else to say. Suddenly, all I wanted to do was get out of his line of sight. I turned and left without another word.

As I was walking along the hallway that led back to the entryway, Zach came out of the door that led to the ticket office. His long rust-red hair was tied back in a low pony-tail, and his faded jeans and Nightmare Sanctuary T-shirt were tight on his muscular body. "What did you do to him?" Zach asked me.

"I didn't do anything!" I answered. I didn't even have to ask who Zach was talking about.

"I tried to talk to Damien earlier. He's in such a bad mood that I look like a ray of sunshine in comparison!" Zach threw back his head and laughed, just a hint of a werewolf's howl in the sound.

"Well, it's not my fault." I paused, then added, "Please be nice to him. He's…got some stuff going on."

I sound like Mama.

"I'm always nice," Zach said with a goofy grin.

"Mm-hmm. Sure." Zach was easily the grumpiest person at the Sanctuary, since he only got to be a werewolf three days every month. He said he preferred that form to the everyday, human body he was stuck in most of the time.

Zach retreated into the ticket office, and I continued on my way, but I only made it as far as the entryway. Justine was just coming down the stairs, and she hurried down the last few and bounded over to me. "Don't hate me, Olivia," she said in greeting.

I peered at her. "Why?" I asked slowly.

Justine leaned toward me and whispered, "All the temps are going to be paired with someone again tonight. I put Annabelle with you."

My first instinct was to groan, but I could see the logic in Justine's decision. We had promised to make sure Annabelle didn't go to Under the Undertaker's or anywhere else she might run into Callie, and pairing us up was an easy way for me to keep an eye on her.

Justine was watching me anxiously, and I patted her arm. "I don't like it, but I get it."

We walked together toward the dining room as Justine thanked me over and over.

"Who knows?" I said, laughing. "Maybe she and I will become best friends!"

"Ha!" Justine pulled open the dining room door, and we both froze in place.

There was a woman sprawled on the floor right in front of us.

CHAPTER FIVE

Justine reacted much better—and much more quickly—than me. She rushed forward, and even as she was kneeling down next to the woman, the dining room door was slowly closing in front of me. Finally, just before it shut completely, I reached forward and grabbed the handle.

Oh, please, I thought, *not another murder.*

It wasn't. As soon as I stepped over the threshold, I could see the woman's chest rising and falling, the folds of her gauzy peach-colored dress shifting with each inhale. Her face was pale and pinched, but she was probably pretty under ordinary circumstances, like when she wasn't sprawled on the cold stone floor of an old hospital dining room.

"Ow, you're stepping on my hair!" the woman said in a high, whiny voice.

A voice equally high yet much more composed said, "Oh, I'm sorry, Annabelle."

Oh, boy. What an introduction to the notorious fairy.

I looked up and saw the second voice had come from Maida, the youngest of the three witches who lived and worked at the Sanctuary. She looked like she was about ten years old, though she acted like someone much older and wiser. As I watched, she stepped back, moving her old-fashioned black-buttoned ankle boot off Annabelle's long pale-blue hair, which was spread out on the floor around her head like some kind of halo.

"Your aura is all over the place," said Morgan, the oldest witch. She was bent over Annabelle, blinking at her with wide eyes set in a thin, wrinkled face. "What is the nature of your distress?"

"I'm trying to get used to the nocturnal habits you keep here," Annabelle wailed. "I've slept terribly the past few days. Then, the grocery store in this dumb little town didn't have my brand of organic honey, so I'm under-nourished."

Madge glanced at me, and I could see the dislike in her eyes. *Does anyone like Annabelle?* Madge was ordinarily so kind to everyone, but I knew what it looked like when her beautiful face was twisted with rage. I had seen her threaten to unleash her magic on someone who had crossed her, and I wouldn't have wanted to be on her bad side. It seemed like Annabelle was already there.

Madge tossed her long golden curls over her shoulder. Unlike the other two witches, she seemed wholly unconcerned with Annabelle's current state. "There are plenty of other things to eat at that store, and we have a stocked pantry right here."

"But my honey! I need sugar, or I'll faint again!"

"Here!" Maida reached into the patch pocket on the front of her knee-length black dress and pulled out a handful of candy. "It's Halloween candy! It will make you feel better."

"Thank you, child," Annabelle said, reaching up a shaky arm to retrieve the candy.

"Let's get you up first," Justine suggested. "Olivia, can you help?"

I nodded and moved to one side of Annabelle. Justine and I took her by the elbows and helped her up, then escorted her to the nearest bench. Annabelle didn't thank

30

us. Instead, she eagerly unwrapped a miniature candy bar and stuffed the whole thing into her mouth.

Justine turned to me so Annabelle couldn't see her face. "Wow," she mouthed.

I just raised my eyebrows and gave the slightest nod in response.

Since Annabelle didn't seem like she would be fainting again anytime soon, Justine and I moved over to stand with the witches. I leaned down toward Maida. "It was very nice of you to share your candy," I said.

"I thought so," Maida agreed.

"We've taught her to be kind and helpful," Madge said.

"Witches who serve others are less likely to burn at the stake," Morgan added, nodding sagely.

I highly doubted anyone was burned at the stake anymore, but I understood Morgan's point. By that time, other Sanctuary employees were drifting into the dining room, saying hello to us and settling onto benches since it was nearly time for the family meeting.

Theo was already settled in at my usual table when I finally sat down. He wasn't in his zombie pirate costume yet, and he was really handsome without all the gruesome makeup. His fangs had been filed down by a vampire hunter, but his pale skin gave away his supernatural nature. He smiled at me, his brown eyes glittering with mischief, and whispered, "What drama did I miss?"

I quickly filled him in on Annabelle's fainting spell, and Theo had to clamp a hand over his mouth to keep from laughing. "That's a new one," he said once he had gotten his mirth under control. "She must be trying to up her antics from last year."

Before I could ask what those antics had been, Justine stepped up to the podium to begin the family meeting. I was surprised to see someone else step up next to her. It was a man, probably a decade or so older than my forty-two years. His hairline was beginning to recede, but what hair he still had was thick and wavy. He was dressed in jeans and a button-down plaid shirt, and when I leaned a bit to my left to peer between people seated in front of me, I could see he was wearing brown cowboy boots.

"Before we dive into Sanctuary business," Justine began, "I'd like to introduce Winston Byers. Most of you know him already, but for our new folks, he hosts the Nightmare Fall Festival out at his farm. Since the festival opens tomorrow night with the annual kickoff party, I wanted to let everyone know where they'll be. If I call your name, you'll be working the party tomorrow."

Justine started rattling off a list of names, and I was surprised when I heard my own name called. Since I typically took tickets at the Sanctuary, I had just assumed I would be staying put.

And then I knew exactly why Justine had assigned me to the festival when she said, "Olivia, Annabelle, Theo, and Malcolm, the four of you will be haunting the corn maze."

My heart sank. Once again, I totally understood Justine's desire to pair me with Annabelle. What had me feeling less than enthusiastic wasn't that, but the fact I had to spend Thursday evening inside a maze.

I hated mazes. I had gotten lost in one when I was about nine, and in the thirty-plus years since, I hadn't gotten over the experience. In fact, I hated mazes more than I hated going to haunted houses.

That thought cheered me a bit. I had once been worried that my severe dislike of haunted house attractions would keep me from being able to work at the Sanctuary. It had been the first job I could find when I had arrived in Nightmare, and I had been so broke I had to take the risk. Luckily, I had discovered that being the one doing the scaring was a lot of fun. Maybe working a maze would feel different than being lost in one.

Once Justine finished listing the assignments for those of us working the party, Winston stepped up to the podium and said a few nice things about how his farm and the Sanctuary had enjoyed working together on the party every year for more than a decade. He had a drawl that rivaled Tanner's.

After Winston finished, Justine moved on to that night's work at the Sanctuary. I had already known Annabelle would be shadowing me, and I wondered how many times she would faint while taking tickets. I also wondered if I should stuff the pockets of my jeans with Halloween candy, so I could produce a piece anytime she started feeling lightheaded.

Theo still had to get into his pirate costume and put on his zombie makeup, so he made a hasty exit after the meeting wrapped up. He did, however, kiss me on the cheek and wish me luck with what he referred to as "the very dramatic fairy."

I stuck around to chat with Mori and Malcolm. Annabelle had disappeared, and I figured she could find her own way to the entrance.

Sure enough, when I got up there, Annabelle was already standing in the open doorway, smiling coyly at the two men at the front of the line. "Hey, Annabelle," I said as I walked up. "You can grab a Sanctuary T-shirt from the costume room. You want me to point you in the right direction?"

Annabelle wrinkled her nose. "I'm not going to wear black. Ew. So morbid. Besides, this dress looks great on me. These two guys just said so." She lifted her long dress slightly and twirled around.

"Anyone not in a costume should be in a Sanctuary

shirt, so guests know they can ask us questions," I pointed out.

"I don't work here full-time, so I won't have answers to people's questions, anyway," Annabelle said dismissively.

I clenched my jaw so I wouldn't retort. For the sake of Callie, I needed to be nice enough to Annabelle that she wouldn't ask to be paired with someone else. Instead, I said, "Since there's a line already, we can go ahead and start letting guests inside so they can queue."

"Let me guess," Annabelle said, speaking to me but smiling at the two men she had been flirting with. "I take their tickets and let them in?"

"You'll tear off the stub, which you can drop in the bin behind the door. Guests can keep the rest of the ticket as a souvenir."

Annabelle was so busy looking at the men that she tore their tickets right in half, rather than tearing along the perforated line of the ticket stub. They didn't seem to mind, though they were reluctant about stepping past her and winding their way back and forth inside the entryway queue.

"We'd rather stay here and help you," one of them said wistfully.

"Have a spooky time, gentlemen," I said pointedly, and they both sighed.

The next hour was much the same. Annabelle would flirt with any man who looked like he was in his twenties or early thirties, and she would practically ignore everyone else. We soon had a routine going: she tore tickets for the younger guys, and I tore tickets for the other ninety percent of people who were coming through the entrance.

At least, I told myself, *she's helping a little bit.*

Our odd system was interrupted when I felt a brush against my shoulder blade and got that eerie sensation that only happened when someone has snuck up behind you. I heard Damien's voice in my ear. "Would you please come to my office?"

I turned to ask why and saw Damien was wearing his sunglasses. That told me enough, and I immediately said to Annabelle, "I've got something I need to take care of. You've got this!"

"I sure do!" Annabelle said brightly as she beamed at a guy wearing a fraternity T-shirt.

Damien was already on his way back to his office, and I hurried to catch up. Instead of sitting down behind his expansive oak desk, though, he started pacing on the threadbare rug in front of the fireplace. Once I was inside with him, he said, "I don't know what to do."

"About what?"

Damien stopped pacing and leaned against the mantel. "Whether to listen to my father or my mother."

Mama had been right. Damien was torn and probably scared, and I was going to have to help him if he was ever going to make a decision.

"Lucille's message at the séance was about both of us," I said. "Mama heard her voice the night before I arrived in Nightmare, telling her to welcome the stranger. She wants both of us to work on our supernatural skills."

"How do you know you're the stranger my mother was talking about?"

"Mama said she just knew as soon as I walked in the front door of the motel. She's not a powerful psychic like Lucille was, but she's more perceptive than most people."

"So my mother wants both of us to find out what we're capable of." Damien's hand curled into a fist.

"Yes. Mama is convinced that you and I are going to have to hone our abilities and work together to find your father."

"I don't even know what my abilities are. What if I can't control them?"

35

I took a tentative step toward Damien, reaching out a hand but not quite touching his arm. "That's why I'm going to help you. I'll be with you, every step of the way."

Damien turned away from the mantel and faced me. "That's what I'm worried about." He moved until we were so close I had to tilt my face upward to stare at my double reflection in his mirrored sunglasses. I could feel the warmth radiating from him. My heart did a panicked little flip as he lowered his head, our faces just inches apart. "I'm afraid I'm going to hurt you."

CHAPTER SIX

He's going to kiss me, I thought wildly.

That was followed by a thought that was just as unexpected. *I really wish he would take off those infernal sunglasses.*

And then Damien *did* take off his sunglasses.

Did I just conjure that? My brain was going a thousand miles an hour, and it felt like my heart was trying to keep up with it.

Damien taking his sunglasses off only made things worse because that meant I was staring right into his eyes.

"Olivia," Damien began.

I didn't know what Damien was about to say, but I was saved from having to find out because I heard Malcolm's voice behind me. "It's time for your break, Olivia."

I whirled around, heat rushing into my cheeks, but Malcolm didn't look at all shocked by the scene. If he had noticed anything, then he wasn't acting like it.

"Annabelle said you were in here," he added.

Zach was standing right behind Malcolm, but he, too, appeared not to notice the weird vibe between Damien and me. Instead, he looked annoyed. He lifted a hand, a piece of paper clutched in it. "Damien, I've got a group at the window who says they worked out a discount with us, but I have no record of it."

Damien had already slid his sunglasses back on when I

looked at him again. "Enjoy your break," he said to me. With that, he turned and moved behind his desk. I knew I had been dismissed when he sat down and immediately gestured for Zach to come in.

I half expected Malcolm to say something about how close Damien and I had been standing as we walked together down the hallway. When he remained silent, I took the opportunity to think about something that *wouldn't* make me blush. "Did you know Lucille well?" I asked.

Malcolm smiled sadly. "Yes. Baxter was like a big brother to me, and I loved Lucille as a sister. She always accepted me, and she never once judged me or my past."

"You've known Baxter for a long time," I speculated. "But you've never discovered what kind of supernatural creature he is?"

"No. I only know that he's very powerful."

We had neared the entryway, so before we reached the queue of guests, I stopped and looked at Malcolm. "Then do you think Damien is dangerous? If both of his parents were so powerful..." I was beginning to understand Damien's fear of his own potential.

Malcolm was quiet for a few moments, his eyes gazing at a spot on the wall behind me. "We're all dangerous in our own ways," he said eventually. "But, considering Damien's parents, he could well be more dangerous than all the rest of us. However, I caution you from equating supernatural power with danger. Baxter used his for good. He created this haven. This Sanctuary."

I nodded. "I just have to convince Damien that he can explore his power without accidentally"—I waved my hands in the air—"blowing up this town, or whatever it is he's afraid of."

He's afraid of hurting me, a little voice said in my head.

"Go enjoy your break," Malcolm said gently. "Try to

enjoy the Halloween revelry instead of trying to figure out Damien. The latter will only frustrate you."

"Wise words, Malcolm. I'll grab Annabelle."

But when I moved toward the front doors to do just that, I saw that Annabelle was ignoring the people waiting to get inside. She was half-turned away from them, her attention focused on Winston. Their faces were nearly as close together as mine and Damien's had just been, and I instantly wondered if he was flirting with her, or vice versa.

Winston glanced up as I approached, said something to Annabelle in such a low voice that I couldn't hear him, then slid past her out the door.

"Creep," Annabelle said under her breath as he disappeared.

"You okay?" I asked, instinctively reaching out to take the tickets of the people who were waiting to get in. The queue inside the entryway was half empty, which meant Annabelle had been shirking her duties for pretty much the entire time I had been gone.

Great. She's going to be a fantastic co-worker at the festival's kickoff party tomorrow, especially if there's something weird between her and the guy running it.

"I'm fine," Annabelle answered. "He was just saying hello since I worked at the festival last year, too."

I didn't believe for one second that Winston had just been saying hello. Still, it wasn't my business, and I didn't want to get involved in any of Annabelle's drama. Well, not any more than I already had.

"Some sugary snacks are what you need," I said, trying to sound friendly but probably failing miserably. "Malcolm will man the door while we get a quick break."

Once we were in the dining room and I had a bag of potato chips in front of me, I felt more in a mood to be genuinely friendly to Annabelle. I would probably never like her, but I could tolerate her a whole lot better while I was crunching away on something tasty.

"Did you know anyone here in Nightmare before you worked the Halloween season last year?" I asked.

Annabelle gulped down a big bite of chocolate-chip cookie. "Nope."

That meant she wasn't going to admit to knowing Callie, so I tried a different tack. "Where do you live?"

"Differ." Annabelle was talking around another bite of cookie, and it took me a moment to realize she had said "Denver."

"I'm a little envious. We didn't get a lot of snow in Nashville, but I'm sure going to miss it this winter."

"I just don't get why anyone would want to live in this town." Annabelle pursed her lips. "I went to school in Phoenix, which was fine since it's a big city with lots to do. This place is just a dusty little town in the desert."

I had thought the exact same thing when I first arrived in Nightmare, and I cringed to think how judgmental I had been of the quirky little town. After getting settled in—and getting used to the idea that supernatural creatures existed —I had come to really enjoy Nightmare. Even the touristy Wild West reenactments on High Noon Boulevard were charming in my eyes.

Before I could speak up in defense of Nightmare, though, Annabelle let out a shriek and clutched her cookie so tightly it crumbled onto the table. She jumped up from the bench we were sitting on. "Get away from me, you freak!"

I followed Annabelle's line of sight down to the floor, where Felipe was sitting on his haunches and looking up at Annabelle hopefully. His fangs gleamed white against his muzzle.

Felipe shrank back at Annabelle's shouting, and he let out a whimper.

"He just wants some of your snack," I said. "Come here, Felipe. I have some cookies, too." I tore open the package, broke off a piece of chocolate-chip cookie, and held it toward him.

Felipe eyed Annabelle warily as he made a wide circle around her. He jumped up onto the bench next to me so I was between the two of them, then gingerly accepted my peace offering.

Mori swept toward us, her silky mauve gown swirling around her legs. Her blood-orange eyes were flashing. "He wasn't going to hurt you."

Annabelle glared at Mori. "I told you last year that I can't stand ugly little blood-suckers," she spat.

I nearly choked on my potato chip. It was appalling to hear someone speak so disrespectfully to Mori, and Annabelle was clearly directing her comment toward the vampire rather than the chupacabra.

"That's funny, because when you were here last October, you didn't seem to think *I* was ugly." Theo had snuck up on us, which he excelled at doing. I looked over to see him giving Annabelle a look that dared her to contradict him. Of course, with his zombie makeup, he actually did look ugly.

Theo and Mori were two of the people who had made me feel the most welcome when I had started working at the Sanctuary. At the time, none of us had known I had any supernatural ability at all. For that matter, I was unaware that supernatural creatures even existed. I just thought the Sanctuary's employees had really convincing costumes. The two vampires had accepted me and been friendly right from the start, and the fact neither of them liked Annabelle spoke volumes about how intolerable she was.

Annabelle wisely didn't rise to Theo's challenge.

Instead, she huffed out a breath and said, "So much for my break," and stomped out of the room.

Mori turned to me the second Annabelle was out of earshot. "Be careful, Olivia. She's trouble."

"Oh, I've already figured that out," I assured her.

"No, I mean real trouble." Mori sat down on the bench next to me, her dress rustling softly. "She just about got a local boy killed last year, so you watch your step around her."

"Killed? What happened?"

"I don't know all the details, but there were rumors swirling about it for weeks after she left town last year. If I hung out with any of the locals, I would probably know more about it."

"I'll ask Mama," I said, nodding. "She tends to know the town gossip."

Mori smiled. "You tell her I said hello, and that I want to see her. It's been ages."

"I will. She's been nervous that her former friends here are mad that she stopped coming around."

"Former, nothing." Mori sniffed. "I've always adored Sue, and I still consider myself her friend."

"She'll be glad to hear that."

"I tried to ask her out once," Theo said. "She was in her early twenties, and she had the biggest hair I'd ever seen."

I laughed. "She still has big hair! I expect it wasn't gray back then, though. But you said you tried to ask her out. Did she turn you down?"

"She sure did," Theo struck a dramatic pose, the back of one hand pressed against his forehead. "Some guy named Benny beat me to it."

Hearing the affection both Mori and Theo had for Mama made my spirits rise, and I went back to my post at the front door, feeling much more upbeat than I had all night.

When I caught sight of the entrance, I got a sense of déjà vu. Winston was standing there again, talking intently to Annabelle while a line of guests waited for her to take their tickets.

I had thought Winston had left when he had walked out earlier, but obviously, he had doubled back.

I was already mentally composing a lecture when Annabelle jumped back from Winston, her hands curled into fists. "I told you, I'm not interested!" she shrieked. "Get away from me, you creep!"

CHAPTER SEVEN

My first thought wasn't for Annabelle, or even Winston. It was for the guests, both outside the door and winding through the stanchions inside, who were staring at the spectacle with shocked expressions.

I rushed forward, figuring that, if nothing else, I could herd Annabelle and Winston somewhere away from the guests. Zach reached them at the same time I did, and I knew he must have heard the racket from his spot at the ticket window.

Zach grabbed Winston's arm, and Winston immediately tried to take a step back. Unfortunately for him, Zach was a lot stronger, and his grip didn't budge.

"I didn't do anything!" Winston shouted. His face was beet red.

Zach jerked his head in the direction of Damien's office, then looked at Annabelle. "You, too. Let's go." With his free hand, Zach grabbed the radio that was clipped to the waistband of his jeans and handed it to me. "Ask Malcolm to cover for me."

The three of them moved away, Annabelle loudly protesting the entire time that the whole thing was unfair. I quickly made a call on the radio, asking for Malcolm to come sell tickets for a while, then began letting people in. As I tore each ticket, I mumbled, "Sorry about that."

I was apologizing for something I hadn't even done.

I turned angrily to pitch a handful of ticket stubs into the bin, but the stubs fluttered to the ground. Surprised, I looked around. The bin had been moved about five feet away. Had Winston kicked it in his anger? Or had Zach knocked into it when he wrangled Winston away from Annabelle? With a huff, I picked up the stubs and moved the bin back into its proper spot.

Once the crop of witnesses to the scene had all made their way into the haunt itself, I began to calm down a bit. The people coming through at the moment didn't know anything had happened, and they were all smiling and excited.

At one point, I glanced over just in time to see Annabelle come back into the entryway, but she went right past me and headed up the stairs instead of returning to her post. She didn't look upset, but her lower lip stuck out in a pout that was so exaggerated it nearly made me laugh.

I kept one eye on the hallway to Damien's office after that, but I never saw him or Winston. Since Winston ran the Nightmare Fall Festival, I expected Damien was doing everything he could to smooth things over with him. I still didn't know what had transpired between Winston and Annabelle, but I knew the situation couldn't be good.

Zach had returned to the ticket window at some point, and I tried to read his expression, but it was to no avail. His everyday grumpy face was too similar to his "something bad just happened" grumpy face.

The second the last guest of the night had filed past me, I shut the door and made a beeline for the ticket office. Zach had already closed the ticket window, and he was counting through a pile of cash. "Damien and Winston are still in there together," I said.

"Twenty-nine, thirty, thirty-one..." Zach said pointedly.

While I impatiently waited for him to finish his tally, Theo joined us. He had taken off his pirate costume and zombie makeup, but as usual, he still had black streaks around his eyes. It made him look like he was in a rock band or going for some kind of goth look.

"I heard about Annabelle's little outburst," Theo said. Normally, he would enjoy hearing gossip, but he seemed to realize this wasn't one of those occasions. His voice was tense. "How bad was it?"

"I'm waiting on Damien and Winston to get done so I can find out what happened," I said.

"You won't. At least, not tonight." Zach was putting the cash into a lock box, and he shook his head grimly. "Winston was really upset about Annabelle embarrassing him like that, so I expect Damien is still trying to calm him down. Or, more likely, they broke out the brandy that Baxter always kept in the office."

It was pointless to stand around and wait, especially since I knew Damien would be in a rotten mood by the time he was done. Plus, my bed was calling my name. It had turned into a mentally trying day.

"I'm going home," I announced. "I'm working the corn maze at the festival kickoff tomorrow, so I'll see you two on Friday."

Theo elbowed me playfully. "I'm working there with you, remember?"

I smiled. "Oh, yeah. I'm so tired I forgot. That makes me feel better. Good night."

Zach waved, and Theo said, "Keep an eye out for Mori on your way home. She took Felipe out for a snack since he was so upset about being yelled at."

"Poor boy," I said quietly as I walked away.

By the time I went to bed that night, I was worried about Damien but for a completely different reason than the day before. I was also anxious to know what had happened in the aftermath of that bizarre exchange between Annabelle and Winston, and I was even feeling sorry for Felipe. If someone had told me, back when I was living a normal life in Nashville, that I would someday lose sleep because of a sad chupacabra, I would have thought it was a joke.

Sleep was elusive, and after tossing and turning until about nine in the morning, I finally gave up and crawled out of bed. All the same things were still on my mind, but I also had a distinct feeling of dread since the Nightmare Fall Festival's kickoff party was looming. I was so not looking forward to it.

The fact I was dreading a party only added to my gloomy mood. Ordinarily, I would have looked forward to the chance to work at a party, especially one held outside in the fresh air on a crisp fall evening. And while I wasn't the type of person who went all out for Halloween, I did like the holiday. My ex-husband, Mark, and I had never gotten many trick-or-treaters at our house, but I had enjoyed the excited smiles and fun costumes of the kids who did come up and ring the doorbell.

There was nothing I could do about the evening ahead of me, and I assumed Felipe's mood had improved after getting what Theo had referred to as a snack. Chupacabras were called goat-suckers for good reason, but Mori had once told me goats were hard to come by in Nightmare. When she and Felipe had once stayed with me for a few nights, Felipe had devoured a tray of ground beef that I had in my fridge—literally, he ate both the meat and the Styrofoam tray—and I hoped his "snack" the night before had been something equally sedate.

Of all the things I was worrying about, there was only one I could tackle. After I'd showered, dressed, and had my first cup of coffee, I called Damien. Not surprisingly, my call went to his voicemail. I was undaunted, though, so I climbed into my clunker of a car and drove to the one place I thought he might be: Sonny's Folly Mine.

Baxter had bought the disused copper mine and turned it into a home. The whole place was warded against supernatural creatures, and it had been a way of keeping Lucille safe—both from herself and the outside world—as her psychic powers grew dangerously strong.

The rusted iron door of the mine clanged loudly as I knocked, and I was relieved to hear a similar clang just a few seconds later. Damien was unlocking the door. As the door swung open, I could see Damien's bleary eyes and unkempt hair. Judging by his haggard look, he had slept even worse than me.

"I knew it," Damien said in greeting.

"Knew what?" I asked, moving inside as Damien stepped back.

"That you wouldn't take the hint when I didn't answer your call."

"I'm worried about you. Is that so bad?" I stopped short, and my jaw dropped open. "Wow."

The front part of the mine was a spacious area that had been hewn out of the rock. Baxter had turned it into a living room, while the bedrooms were down the two tunnels that led off of it. Damien had been making updates to the place. The glaring overhead sodium lights had been replaced with floor lamps that gave the room a cozier feel. Even the reddish rock walls seemed softer, and they had a golden glow thanks to the new lights.

The furniture had been updated, too. The old sofa and worn leather chair were gone, replaced by a gorgeous brown leather sectional.

"I was trying to find a place to live, but nothing really did it for me," Damien said as he shut the door with a clang. "Since I apparently lived here as a baby, according to Mama, I figured I'd make it my home again."

"This is good," I said, nodding. "I heard your father's voice here, and we know your mother lived here. The closer of a tie you have to them, the better you'll be able to explore the supernatural abilities they passed on to you."

"I thought the same, actually."

I felt one corner of my mouth turn up in a smile, but I wasn't going to celebrate just yet. Tentatively, I asked, "Does that mean you've decided to train with me?"

Damien furrowed his brow. "I didn't say that."

I could see I wasn't going to get anywhere with that point, so I brought up the reason I had come to the mine in the first place. "I was worried about you after what happened last night. Is Winston very mad?"

Instead of answering me, Damien stalked over to one wall, where a small kitchen had been installed. It had yet to be updated, and two of the wooden cabinet doors were hanging by just one hinge. The countertop and sink, at least, were clean. Damien swept a plate and a coffee cup off the countertop and into the sink, then started moving clean dishes from a dish rack into a cabinet. I had never seen someone put away dishes so aggressively.

Winston had been very mad, then.

"I'm sorry you had to diffuse that situation," I said lamely.

Damien slammed the cabinet door shut and braced himself on the counter. "That fairy nearly cost us thousands of dollars. I should have fired her on the spot."

CHAPTER EIGHT

"Fired her?" I repeated, incredulous. "She wasn't behaving at all professionally, but if Winston was hitting on her, then maybe she felt she needed to be firm with him."

I can't believe I'm defending Annabelle.

Damien turned away from the kitchen cabinets and gave me a curious look. "Firm? First of all, shouting is not being firm. Second, Winston wasn't hitting on her."

"Oh. I just assumed... I mean, that's kind of what it looked like, and since she started yelling..."

"According to what they both told me in my office, Winston was offering her a job. She worked for him part-time last season, doing things around the festival each afternoon before starting her work for us in the evening."

"Yeah, Daniel had told me about that." I moved to the lush new couch and sank down into it. It was a lot more comfortable than the old, seventies-era one that had been there before. Damien came over and sat down next to me as I said, "But, if he was offering her the job again this year, why did she yell at him? She even called Winston a creep!"

"Winston was offering Annabelle a full-time job this year. He wanted her to quit the Sanctuary and devote all of her time to the fall festival."

"That still doesn't explain why she reacted so violently,"

I said. There had to be more to the story. Why would anyone get so upset over a job offer?

"It makes sense if you know anything about fairies."

I spread my hands. "Which I obviously don't. I've never thought to ask Clara about... What would you even call it? Fairy culture?"

Damien almost smiled at that.

"That works," he said. "Fairies tend to make people feel good. You enjoy being around Clara, right?"

"Yeah, she's great. She's always so upbeat and energetic."

"Exactly. Part of that is Clara's personality—she really is one of the good ones—but it's also because she's a fairy. Even humans who don't know the supernatural world exists are affected by what some people call the ethereal glow."

I frowned. "I've never seen Clara glow."

"It's rare for a fairy to actually glow. My father said he's only ever met one fairy who radiated light. It's more about their energy."

I nodded in understanding. "Like their aura. Even if you can't see it, you can feel it. Fairies emanate energy that feels good." Just like Mama could feel a person's vibes, as she called them, people could feel the good feelings fairies gave off.

"Right. And, for centuries, fairies have been sought after by people who want to bask in that glow. They want fairies around them because their very presence makes them feel good."

"And I'm guessing the fairies weren't always given a choice in the matter," I said.

"Long ago, there were people called collectors. They caught fairies and sold them to the highest bidder."

I brought both hands to my mouth. "That's horrible," I said around my fingers.

"It is. And it's one of the reasons fairies get wary whenever someone talks about hiring them for something. Fairy folk see it as a potential trap. Which is why, when fairies find a person or an employer who values them for who they are, and not how they make people feel, they're fiercely loyal."

"And Winston wanted Annabelle to break her loyalty to the Sanctuary, which she would have considered a betrayal," I said. "Annabelle probably noticed how closely he was standing to her and thought he was enjoying her earthy glow, or whatever you called it."

"Ethereal glow. And yes, I think that's exactly what happened. She realized Winston liked the way she made him feel, even though he didn't know it had a supernatural origin. Of course, Annabelle couldn't talk about fairy history in front of Winston, but she said enough that I understood why she reacted so badly to his offer. Still, she could have told him off quietly instead of making such a big scene."

"Agreed. But, she does seem to enjoy calling attention to herself in the most dramatic fashion possible. He offered her a job, and in turn, she humiliated him in front of a crowd of people. And I imagine Winston had a hard time understanding her ire, since he's not in the know."

"It took me hours, plus a lot of my father's brandy, to calm him down. He even threatened to kick us out of the festival, but we need the ticket sales and the publicity we get from being there, so I made sure he agreed to continue our partnership. We sell so many tickets at our festival booth every year."

"Well, Damien, I was already dreading the festival tonight, so it can't get much worse. I'll keep an eye on her while we're there. There will be no embarrassing scenes at the kickoff party!"

"Use your conjuring skills. Focus your thoughts on how much you want Annabelle to not be a problem tonight."

I laughed. "Oh, no, I've learned my lesson! The last time I did that, I thought I had conjured Leonard Evers's murder. Now, I know I have to be very clear and specific in what I want to conjure. I'll focus my wishes on Annabelle, but it will be that she's kind and helpful throughout the evening. It will be a good exercise, not just to hone my conjuring skills, but also to try to forget that I'm inside a maze." I suppressed a shudder, but Damien didn't seem to notice my discomfort. He rose and wandered toward the small round table in one corner of the room. It was piled with moving boxes.

I tried to convince Damien that he should be training, too, but he dismissed that idea by pointedly ripping the tape off the top of a box. When I left, he was elbow deep in the box and didn't even say goodbye.

Rude, or just scared? I gave myself a little shake as I walked out into the sunshine, like I could fling off any pieces of Damien's grim mood that might have stuck to me.

Maybe I just need a fairy to make me feel good. Damien's explanation didn't excuse Annabelle's behavior toward Winston, and I made a mental note to be extra-special nice to him that night at the festival.

We had to report to the festival at six o'clock that evening, with the festivities scheduled to start at seven. The kickoff party would only be two hours long, so I would get home well before the Sanctuary closed for the evening. I could go to bed at a normal hour. That was the little carrot I was mentally dangling in front of myself as I drove to the festival. *Just two hours of work, then you can go to bed at a decent time.*

Winston's farm was only about three miles outside of Nightmare, but it felt like an entirely different world. After

I drove gently uphill for about a mile, the landscape changed to rolling hills dotted by fields. I would have enjoyed the scenery more if it had been full daylight, but even in the last glow of the day, the area looked serene.

I turned left at a dirt road with two signs next to it. One read *Byers Farm, Est. 1983*, and the other had a grinning jack-o'-lantern painted on it along with the words *Nightmare Fall Festival*. The dirt road led to a makeshift parking lot, which appeared to be a cow pasture at other times of the year. I had to watch my step as I walked toward a cluster of pavilions that had been set up near a big red barn. Floodlights had been set high on poles to illuminate the area.

There had been about two dozen cars in the parking lot, so I wasn't surprised to find a bustling scene as I drew closer to the pavilions. There were bales of hay stacked around the area for people to sit on, and of course, there was a pumpkin patch at one side.

The white pavilions held everything from food vendors to carnival games, and every single one of them had been trimmed with dried corn stalks and burnt-orange ribbon. People were busy putting up the last of the decorations, and a young woman sailed past me with a burlap ghost dangling from her raised hand.

The smell of smoke hit me, and I turned to see a few people getting a bonfire started in the middle of the festival space. Nearby, someone was neatly arranging caramel apples on a folding table covered with a purple-and-black striped tablecloth.

The whole scene was so quaint—the epitome of a harvest festival out in farm country—that I actually felt excitement overcoming my dread. I wanted nothing more than to sprawl on one of the hay bales and sink my teeth into a sticky-sweet caramel apple.

Most of the people around me were clearly on their

way somewhere else, but I realized one of them was heading right for me. It was Winston, who looked harried but pleased. "What do you think?" he asked.

"I think it's perfect," I answered honestly.

Winston looked past me. "Kenzie! Come on over here!" he shouted.

In a moment, we were joined by a woman who looked like she was in her late twenties or early thirties. She had pulled her brown hair up into a bun with a pencil, and her disheveled T-shirt proclaimed she was part of the fall festival staff.

"Kenzie," Winston said, "this is…"

"Olivia," I supplied.

"Yes. From Nightmare Sanctuary Haunted House. She'll be your main point of contact for anything you need from those folks. Olivia, Kenzie here is my assistant manager, and she knows all the ins and outs of this place."

"Come on," Kenzie said, skipping past any pleasantries and getting right down to business. "I'll show you to the dressing room. We've got costumes for those of you who will be in the maze."

The "dressing room" turned out to be an old horse stall inside the barn. Work lights had been clipped to the top edge of the stall, and I was relieved to see the floor was cleaner than the parking lot had been. Kenzie pointed out several options for costumes, told me to have fun with the box full of Halloween makeup, and said she'd meet me and the rest of the Sanctuary staff at our booth at six thirty.

Everyone else would be arriving together, carpooling from the Sanctuary. I took advantage of the momentary privacy to throw on a costume. Since I was the first arrival, I was able to snag the black floor-length dress that was covered with tattered lace. I felt both elegant and spooky. After rummaging through the makeup box, I gave myself a deathly pale face and greenish patches on my cheeks that vaguely resembled mold.

I had been leaning over to put on my makeup, using a tiny mirror hanging on the side of the stall to see what I was doing. When I stood up straight, I heard a shriek.

"You scared me!" Annabelle shouted in her high voice.

"Good!" I grinned at her. "I'm supposed to look scary."

Malcolm and Theo were right behind Annabelle, and I saw Theo roll his eyes in Annabelle's direction.

"Is everyone here?" I asked Malcolm.

"Yes. Two of the temps, Daniel and Sam, are getting the booth set up with all of our flyers and coupons." He reached up and smoothed the collar of his long black coat. "Those of us haunting the maze are supposed to put on a costume, but I doubt anything piled in a horse stall will beat my look."

"You do have the advantage of always being dressed for fright," I assured him.

"I brought my outfit with me." Theo lifted an arm, and I saw that he had brought his pirate costume.

"That means I get to pick anything here!" Annabelle started forward eagerly, then paused with the fingers of one hand curled around a burgundy skirt. "You boys get out. I need to change."

I got out, too, walking with Malcolm and Theo over to the Nightmare Sanctuary booth. I hadn't seen much of Daniel since I had worked with him at the front entrance of the Sanctuary on Tuesday night. As soon as he spotted me, he stopped arranging brochures on the table and leaned toward me. "I hear I missed some ticket-taking drama last night!"

"Ugh," was all I responded.

Kenzie, the assistant manager, came over to meet with us right at the promised time. By then, Annabelle had joined us. She was in the middle of twirling around so we could admire her long skirt and corset top, and all of us—except Annabelle—were happy to switch our attention to Kenzie. She gave us a quick briefing, telling us to spread out in the maze and to take it easy on the younger kids. Soon, I was following Malcolm, Theo, and Annabelle into a maze cut into a small cornfield.

Annabelle was the first to take up a post as we wandered into the maze, picking a spot a couple turns in. Several turns later, Malcolm suggested I hide in a dark corner. I watched him and Theo disappear into the shadows as I wished we were using the buddy system for this assignment.

I relaxed a bit once seven o'clock rolled around. People were laughing and screaming as they made their way through the maze, clearly enjoying themselves. As I focused on scaring them, I forgot about my discomfort.

A high, girlish giggle sounded somewhere near me, and I instantly knew it was Annabelle. She must have wandered away from her post if I was able to hear her.

I sighed. I had promised Damien I would keep an eye on Annabelle in an attempt to avoid more conflict with Winston, so I set off in the direction of the giggling. Every few seconds, I would hear it, and it got louder as I got closer to her.

The giggling was louder than ever when it turned into a choked gurgle.

Then I heard nothing but silence.

CHAPTER NINE

My fear of being inside the maze instantly turned into fear that something had happened to Annabelle. I started to run. Judging by the closeness of the sound, she was just around the next corner.

Except she wasn't. I rounded the corner at full tilt and saw no one. Twenty feet later, I hit a dead end. I turned back and retraced my steps to the nearest branch in the path. I turned onto it and continued to run. The path looped back on itself, and as I made the turn, I saw something on the ground just in front of me.

There wasn't a lot of light that deep in the maze, but I knew without a doubt it was Annabelle. Someone was crouched over her, a man who had one hand wrapped around her wrist. He looked up at me. "Call nine-one-one," he demanded, "then go find a staff member and tell them we have a medical emergency."

I made the call on my cell phone as I tried to find my way out of the maze. I took three wrong turns and knocked into a party of giggling teenagers, but eventually, I was at the entrance. By then, I was off the phone, and I quickly scanned the crowd. I spotted Winston walking toward the dunk tank, and I ran forward, shouting his name.

Quickly, I told Winston something had happened to

Annabelle and that an ambulance was on the way. He was moving before I finished, and in moments, he had told the person manning the maze entrance to stop letting people in, and he disappeared into the rows of corn.

I stood there, feeling breathless and stunned.

At least I don't have to worry that I conjured a murder.

I instantly chastised myself for such a selfish thought. *Besides, maybe Annabelle isn't dead,* I told myself. But she was. I could tell by the way she had been lying there on the ground. It wasn't a natural position, and her head had lolled at a strange angle.

Annabelle had been giggling, but at what? She must have been with someone who was making her laugh, but the only person I saw near her was the person who had told me to call an ambulance. Had he been her killer and he was only pretending to help?

Since the maze was already open to the public, anyone could have slipped in and... Well, I wasn't sure what they had done, but I knew it had ended with Annabelle making that horrible gurgling noise. Maybe she had been choked to death. That would explain why her giggling had cut off so abruptly. There was no way I wanted a closer look, so I would let the police figure out what had happened.

"So much for a fun Halloween party," I mumbled. My dread about the maze had been justified, but in the most awful way possible.

I still had my phone in my hand, so I called Damien. He needed to know what was happening since it involved one of his temp employees. For that matter, I expected that Theo, Malcolm, and I would all be thoroughly questioned by the police since we had been nearby.

When Damien answered, I breathlessly told him what had happened. "I'm on my way," he said. Then, in a softer tone, he added, "Are you okay?"

"I'm shaken, but I'm fine. Please get here soon."

Knowing Damien was on his way made me feel better, and again, I was struck by how unpredictable our relationship had become. Earlier, he had wanted me out of his new home in the mine. Now, he was asking if I was okay.

I slid my cell phone into my pocket and marched over to the staff member Winston had told to keep people out of the maze. Two more staff members had joined her, and they stood shoulder-to-shoulder to block the entrance between two rows of corn.

"Did anyone come out of here in a hurry?" I asked without preamble. I pointed toward the maze entrance.

"You did," the staff member Winston had spoken to said, one eyebrow raised.

"Yes, because I was looking for help. But before I came out of the maze, was there anyone else? Anyone who looked suspicious?"

All three of the festival staff members turned their heads slowly and gazed into the maze. One by one, they looked back at me with wide eyes. "What happened in there?" one of them asked.

"Someone was…" I stopped and cleared my throat. "A medical emergency. An ambulance is on the way. But I thought maybe you saw something."

"Like what?" The staff member I had initially spoken to crossed her arms. "The exit to the maze is on the other side of the field. No one came out this way except you."

That meant if Annabelle had been killed, her murderer could have slipped right out the exit along with everyone else, looking like just another reveler. Or, they could still be inside the maze at that very moment, pretending to be lost.

Distantly, I could hear the wail of a siren, and before long, two EMTs with a stretcher came into view. The staff and I waved our arms, and they came toward us.

"Can you show us where to go?" one of the EMTs asked me.

Can I? I hadn't paid any attention to the turns I had taken to get back to the entrance.

Winston came rushing out of the maze at that moment. "I heard the sirens. Thank goodness you're here. Come on." In a flash, he and the EMTs had disappeared inside the maze.

A minute later, Kenzie ran up to us. "No one can leave," she said.

"We have to keep people inside the maze?" I asked, horrified at the idea.

"No one can leave the festival," Kenzie clarified. She waved a radio. "Winston said we need to keep everyone here until the police have had a chance to look around. Staff has been posted at the parking lot. So, if anyone asks, tell them they have to stay, but they can have free popcorn and soda while they wait."

Kenzie sped off to continue spreading the word, and I stared after her, unsure what to do with myself. I didn't want to go back inside the maze, and I knew we were in for a long night. I glanced down at my tattered black dress. *I don't want to be interrogated wearing this.*

I sprinted to the barn, ducked into the makeshift changing room, and quickly changed back into my Sanctuary T-shirt and jeans. The only light in there came from the work lights hanging in the stall, and I felt very lonely and isolated. I wiped at my face with a tissue and managed to get the green spots off, though my reflection in the tiny mirror still looked horribly pale. That probably wasn't only because of the white foundation I hadn't been able to remove.

When I walked out of the barn, I could see more flashing lights. The police had arrived. By that time, a lot of people had gathered around the maze entrance, and I could hear the way everyone was speculating about what had happened.

"Someone got so scared they had a heart attack," I heard one woman say.

Someone else, a teenager by the looks of it, said, "I heard it was one of the freaks from the Sanctuary."

"Freaks? Is that the best you can come up with?" It was Daniel, who had wandered over from the Sanctuary booth to join the throng.

The teenager turned around with his mouth open, clearly about to retort, then caught sight of Daniel's and my matching T-shirts. "Sorry," he mumbled before moving away.

"I guess there's a bonus to people thinking you're one of the strange ones," I commented.

"It was her, wasn't it?" Daniel said quietly.

"Yeah. How did you know?"

He shrugged. "I saw the tall one and the fangless vampire wandering around, Sam has been with me, and you're right here. That only leaves one person. Is she really dead, like some people are saying?"

I hesitated, then nodded. "I don't know what happened, though."

Daniel's shoulders slumped. "I didn't like her, but not enough to wish her dead."

"None of us wished for it," I said, thinking of my efforts to conjure a night of Annabelle being nice and polite.

That's not true, I realized. *Callie wished for it. She literally said she wanted Annabelle to drop dead.*

But Callie was probably serving a drink at Under the Undertaker's at that moment. If this had, in fact, been a murder, then I knew the killer was still there at the festival with us.

I began to scan the crowd, and I saw four police officers moving toward the maze entrance. Damien was following in their wake, so I jostled my way past people as politely as I could to close the distance between us.

Just as I reached Damien, one of the officers turned and caught sight of me. "Oh, no," he moaned.

"Nice to see you, too, Officer Reyes," I said, with just a hint of sarcasm. It wasn't that I disliked Luis Reyes, but he and I only ever saw each other when there was a dead body in town.

"How do you always wind up in the middle of a mur —" Reyes began, then bit his lip. "The middle of a medical situation?"

"I'm just lucky, I suppose."

"Reyes," Damien broke in tightly, "the woman in there is one of the temps who came to help us with the Halloween season. There are some things you should know about her behavior the past few days, and the people involved."

So Damien must suspect Winston of killing her.

Reyes leaned in close to Damien, and I instinctively did the same. In a voice too low to carry to the onlookers, Reyes said, "We haven't even seen her yet. We don't know if this was a homicide. If we determine that it was, then we'll get those details from you."

Before he followed the other officers into the maze, Reyes gave me another look. I had told him I was lucky, but he clearly thought I was some kind of bad-luck charm that had brought murder and mayhem to Nightmare.

It wasn't my fault people kept turning up dead. At least, I didn't think it was.

Damien gave me a hard look. "Are you sure you're okay? You're so pale."

I touched my cheek. "This is just makeup. There was no sink in the stall for me to wash my face."

Damien took me gently by the arm and led me around the

edge of the crowd. He didn't stop until we were out of earshot of the bystanders. We sat down on some hay bales in front of the pumpkin patch, and he said, "Tell me everything."

When I had called Damien, I had told him only that Annabelle was dead. I filled him in on the giggling, and the gurgling, and the man who had been crouched down over her. "He was looking for a pulse at her wrist," I concluded, "but it was pretty obvious he wasn't going to find one. There was no one else around."

"And you think it was murder," Damien said. It was a statement, not a question.

"Annabelle is, what, thirty years old or so? Fairies don't just drop dead at that age. Er, I don't think they do."

"And she doesn't exactly make friends wherever she goes, especially with her flair for the dramatic."

"I thought of Winston, too," I said, guessing where Damien's mind was going with that line of thought. "What's his motive, though? That she yelled at him in front of a bunch of people?"

"Good point. Someone out here with us had a much better motive."

"Agreed. The question is, who?"

I gazed out at the sea of pumpkins in front of me. Something moved to the right of them, and I looked over to see someone walking slowly between the pumpkin patch and the nearest pavilion.

It was Callie.

CHAPTER TEN

She's supposed to be avoiding the fall festival so she won't have to see Annabelle.

I stared at Callie, trying to figure out what she was doing. The floodlights didn't illuminate the path she was treading very well, so she was half in shadow. She reached the edge of the pavilion, not too far from where Damien and I were sitting, then turned and walked back. She disappeared briefly into the shadows, then reappeared, once again heading toward us.

She was pacing back and forth. *Is she worried because she killed Annabelle, and she might get caught?*

Just as I thought that, Callie looked up. Maybe she had felt my eyes boring into her. My chest tightened, like I had just been caught doing something wrong. I jumped up and walked over to Callie, hoping I could make it look more like I was concerned than suspicious.

"Callie, are you all right?" I asked gently.

"I asked you and the other girls to keep her away from me," Callie said in a shaky voice. "I didn't mean like this."

"Callie, you know—"

"I have to go." Callie slid past me, and soon, she had disappeared into the crowd.

I thought about following, but unless I was prepared to outright accuse Callie of murder, there was probably no point. Instead, I headed back to the hay bales, only to find that Damien was gone. It didn't take me long to find him. He and Winston were speaking together a short distance away.

What they were saying was probably none of my business, but I couldn't help myself. I strolled right up to them like they might be having a casual chat about the nice weather.

"…don't need to apologize," Winston was saying as I came within earshot. "It's kind of perfect for Halloween. This is going to reach urban legend status within the week, and people will be flocking here to see the maze. I'm going to make a record amount—"

Winston had spotted me, and he clamped his mouth shut. Apparently, he realized his talk about making a profit off Annabelle's death was inappropriate.

"I understand you found her," Winston said, his tone changing from triumphant to something bordering on sympathetic. "I'm so sorry you had to experience that."

I mumbled my thanks, then Winston gave us a nod and left.

"He said the police are letting people leave," Damien said. "I'll walk you to your car."

"Just as soon as I check on everyone else from the Sanctuary."

As we went in search of Theo, Malcolm, Daniel, and Sam, I told Damien I already had two suspects. "Winston might have killed her for a little publicity, and Clara's sister might have done it for revenge," I said. Just then, I spotted Daniel laughing and chatting with a few people who must have been locals from town. "Make that three suspects. Daniel really didn't like Annabelle, and he was bad-mouthing her before I even met her. She stole that part-time festival job out from under him last year."

I double-checked that Daniel was doing okay, but it

seemed pointless since he was clearly fine. He gave me a wave and told me to enjoy my night. The crowd was moving in the direction of the parking lot, since there was no way the kickoff party was going to pick back up after what had happened. Malcolm and Theo, however, were standing near the popcorn stand.

"It just smells so good," Theo was saying as Damien and I walked up. "We didn't have buttered popcorn when I was human, so I never got to taste it. Sometimes it sucks to be a vampire."

"Nice word choice," Malcolm intoned.

"Careful," Damien cautioned. "You don't want someone to overhear you."

"Olivia," Theo said, ignoring Damien completely, "are you okay? Rumor has it you found her."

"I didn't, as a matter of fact. Someone was there before me. It looked like he was checking her pulse."

"That must have been Doctor Simms," Malcolm said, nodding. "Theo used his excellent vampiric hearing to eavesdrop on the doctor's conversation with the police. He heard choking noises nearby in the maze, so he went to render aid. Of course, he was too late."

"What else did you overhear, Theo?" I asked.

"Not much," Theo said. "The police herded all of us out of the maze in short order."

Malcolm looked toward the maze, his gaunt face sad. "None of us liked her, but we certainly didn't want her to die."

"Or get killed," I added.

Malcolm gave me a faint smile. "Of course you're on the case already."

"I think Olivia is right about this being a murder." Theo gave me an appreciative nod. "Healthy young fairies don't just drop dead."

"I said the same thing!" I said.

"Again, careful what you say," Damien growled, looking around to see if we'd been overheard. No one was nearby, though, so Damien relaxed ever so slightly. "Let's go home."

"Just as soon as we collect Daniel and Sam," Theo said. "We'll be right behind you."

That left just Damien and me to walk to the parking lot together. In the short distance we had to cover, he asked me three times if I was okay. After my third time assuring him I was fine, I stopped and looked at him. "Are *you* okay?"

"Yeah, of course." Damien was quiet for a moment, then he added, "If you're too shaken up, I can drive you home. I'll bring you back tomorrow to get your car."

"Thanks, but I don't want to leave my car here overnight. Winston might die of embarrassment if that old thing is sitting out in the middle of his pasture."

We reached my car, and I already had the door open when Damien said, "Olivia?"

"Yes?"

"You didn't kill her with your conjuring skills."

"I know," I reassured him. "I'm learning how to set my intentions so I won't have anything like that on my conscience. You should train, too, so you can have the same peace of mind." I slid into the driver's seat and shut the door before Damien could retort.

I was so busy thinking about Annabelle's murder that I completely missed the turn for the road back to Nightmare. I was half a mile past it by the time I realized I had no idea where I was. Sometimes, I really missed having a car with GPS.

My dreams that night were full of eerie giggling and an endless maze that I couldn't find my way out of. I woke up on Friday morning to discover I'd kicked off my comforter, and my legs were tangled in the sheet.

I was going to need a lot of coffee.

There were a few small tasks I needed to do for the Cowboy's Corral social media accounts, so I hauled my big old laptop to the front office after I had gotten ready for the day. Which, of course, included sucking down two cups of coffee. My third cup went into my travel mug so I could sip while I worked.

Mama was behind the counter in the office, and she looked up expectantly at the tinkling of the bell over the door. "It's just me," I called as I headed for the most comfortable chair in the lobby. The brown shag carpet was gleaming in the morning sun that streamed through the windows, making it look slightly less out of date.

"You're the one I want to see!" Mama said. She stood up and moved around the counter in a hurry. "You were there, weren't you?"

I put the laptop down as I nodded. "Yeah. I was the second person on the scene. None of us liked her, Mama, but we certainly didn't want her to die." It had been said before, by others, but it was true.

"Of course you didn't," Mama said dismissively. "Now, tell me everything."

My eye fell on a box next to the coffee maker that sat on a small table in the lobby. "I'll talk if you let me have one of whatever's in there."

"Cinnamon rolls, of course." Mama swept up the box and held it toward me as she opened the lid.

I picked up a cinnamon roll, but before taking a single bite, I filled Mama in on the events at the kickoff party.

"What a shame for Winston," Mama said, clicking her tongue. "He counts on the income from the festival to keep his farm afloat."

I barked out a laugh. "Oh, don't feel sorry for him. Winston expects he'll have a bigger crowd than ever once word gets out. And, since this is the tiny, gossip-happy town of Nightmare, I promise you that word is already out."

Mama glanced over her shoulder, toward the south wing of the motel, where my apartment was. "I never thought about using murder for marketing."

"Don't get any ideas!" I said, laughing. I knew she wouldn't really try to capitalize on the murder that had happened almost directly underneath my apartment.

Just as I bit into my cinnamon roll, Mama said thoughtfully, "It's not really a surprise. That Annabelle girl was trouble."

I raised both eyebrows as I chewed.

"When she was in Nightmare last year, she very nearly got a guy killed," Mama continued.

I swallowed as fast as I could. "Mori mentioned something about that. What happened?"

"I'm not sure, to be honest. I only heard bits of the rumor. You should check with Ella. I think she was involved somehow."

It was a really good thing I hadn't taken another bite, because I probably would have spit it right out in my surprise. "Ella Griffin? The server at The Lusty?"

"Mm-hmm."

"Then I guess I know where I'm going for lunch today."

After I chatted with Mama some more, I finished my cinnamon roll and got to work on the laptop she had loaned me. I couldn't afford to stay at the motel when I had first arrived in Nightmare, but once Mama had found out about my background in marketing, she had offered the apartment in exchange for me doing marketing for the motel. I hadn't expected to wind up living in a tiny mining town in Arizona, and I certainly hadn't expected to find myself juggling two jobs, but the setup worked well for me. I really enjoyed my new life in

Nightmare, when I overlooked the surprising number of murders.

When lunchtime rolled around, I told Mama to wish me luck, stashed my laptop in my apartment, and walked in the direction of The Lusty Lunch Counter. It was still warm out, even though it was the middle of October, but it wasn't oppressive.

My route took me right down High Noon Boulevard, which was the hub of Nightmare tourism. Now that the heat of summer was past, more people were visiting the town to enjoy the Wild West look of the street and the costumed actors who did reenactments. The paved street had been covered over with dirt to make it look more authentic, and the air was hazy with dust from all the people walking along it.

I dodged an oncoming stagecoach, which shuttled tourists around, and hopped onto the covered boardwalk on the right side of the street. The shade was nice, even though there was a crowd of people I had to work my way through.

The Lusty Lunch Counter was one street over from High Noon Boulevard, and the difference in the atmosphere there was remarkable. Tourists didn't usually stray off that main road through the old part of town, so I was soon out of the crowds.

There was another dramatic change when I walked through the front door of The Lusty. Outside, the two-story clapboard building looked like something from a ghost town, complete with a high Western-style facade, a tilting balcony, and peeling paint. Inside, it looked like a classic diner, with a shiny stainless steel counter and booths with padded red benches.

I slid up onto a stool at the counter and waved when Ella looked in my direction. She smiled and held up one finger, then ducked through the doors into the kitchen. As I waited for her, I felt someone sit down next to me. I turned and saw it was Officer Reyes. He took off his cap and ran a hand through his reddish-brown hair.

"This is serendipitous," he began. "You're just the person I wanted to see."

"Is it about Annabelle's murder?" I asked in a low voice.

Reyes made a noise that was part chuckle, part exasperation. "And *that's* exactly why I wanted to see you. To tell you that this was, in fact, not a murder. Ms. Yates died of natural causes."

CHAPTER ELEVEN

"Annabelle Yates had an unfortunate cardiac event," Reyes continued. Ella came over to us at that moment, a diet soda for me in her hand. Reyes nodded at her and smiled, like we weren't sitting there discussing death. "Coffee for me, please, Ella."

When Ella had moved off to fill a coffee cup, I said, "Wasn't she a little young to have a cardiac event, as you call it?"

"Certainly, but it's not unheard of." Reyes must have seen the skepticism in my expression, because he added, "I know you said you heard her making a choking sound, but there are no marks on her neck, and no sign of poison. This wasn't murder, Ms. Kendrick."

Oh, boy. Reyes was using *Ms. Kendrick* instead of *Olivia.* That meant he really wanted me to take him seriously. "It's a shame she died, but it's good news that you don't have to look for a killer," I said.

Reyes rapped his knuckles on the countertop firmly, like he was concluding our meeting. "I figured you were already looking into potential suspects, so I wanted to make sure you were one of the first to get the news."

I took a long sip of my soda while Reyes ordered a chicken-fried steak from Ella. I felt strange, almost deflated. I knew I should feel relieved that there wasn't yet another murderer loose in Nightmare, but something about the whole situation didn't seem right to me.

Of course, I wasn't going to tell Reyes that, because he would just warn me to keep my distance. He was probably still holding a grudge that I had gotten his go-to psychic advisor arrested for murder.

Ella hadn't bothered to take my lunch order, because I always got the cheeseburger and fries. Reyes asked a few polite questions while we were waiting on our food, like how the crowds were at the Sanctuary and whether Cowboy's Corral was planning to have a float in the Nightmare Christmas parade.

Our food had arrived, and I was on my third fry when Reyes brought up Annabelle's case again. "And just so you know," he said suddenly, "we're getting a full lab workup done, so we can be sure."

And just in case it was murder, I thought. What I said, though, was, "That's a good idea. I'm sure it will give her family and friends peace of mind to know every possibility was considered."

"Exactly. But back to the Christmas parade. You're going to love it. Last year—" Reyes stopped speaking and sat up stiffly. He dropped the steak knife in his hand, and it clattered onto the plate.

I followed his gaze and saw that Winston and his assistant manager, Kenzie, had just come through the front door. Both of them were staring hard at Reyes.

A party of four was leaving, and they walked right through the middle of the stare-off that was happening. That seemed to break the tension some, and by the time the party had left, Winston and Kenzie were heading in the direction of a booth. They sat as far from the counter— and from Reyes—as possible.

"Are they unhappy with you?" I asked.

"Last night, we didn't know whether the death was

intentional or accidental. We, uh, were very thorough in our questioning." Reyes cleared his throat and began to attack his chicken-fried steak with his knife. "Not everyone likes being part of an investigation."

Ouch. Was that another dig at me? It wasn't that I liked being involved in murder investigations. It was more that I liked knowing the truth, and I could be pretty determined to track that truth down.

Determined. Or stubborn. Both words sort of worked.

I threw a quick glance over my shoulder, toward the booth where Winston and Kenzie were sitting, their heads close together in conversation. I had been on the receiving end of Reyes's questioning the time someone had mistakenly identified me as their attacker. It wasn't pleasant, and I could understand how Winston and Kenzie might still be feeling the sting.

Reyes turned the subject back to the parade, but I could tell he was straining to make small talk. Finally, he gave up trying and focused on his lunch, and we sat in silence for a while. I was just taking the last bite of my cheeseburger when I heard a muffled sob behind me, and I looked over my shoulder to see Kenzie running out of the diner, her head down and her hands held over her face. Somehow, she made it outside without tripping or running into anything, which was impressive.

No sooner was she out the door than I saw Winston walking toward us. Reyes turned on his stool to face him, and once again, I could see the way he stiffened.

"This is your fault," Winston hissed, stabbing a finger against Reyes's chest. "You made her feel so guilty that she can't even eat her lunch in the same place as you."

"I was just doing my job," Reyes said in an even tone.

"You made her feel like she was on trial for murder!" Winston looked like he wanted to say more, but he wisely turned and left, stomping his way out of the diner while everyone watched, soaking up every bit of the drama.

Reyes slowly turned to face the counter again. "Like I said, some people can't take the questioning."

"Maybe there's something she feels guilty about, and you hit a little too close to home," I suggested carefully.

Reyes sighed. "I wanted to get witness statements last night, while the events of the evening were still fresh in everyone's minds. I had just sat down to eat dinner when they called me to come help, and we had a lot of people to talk to. I was hungry, I was in a hurry, and I was in a bad mood. It's possible I was a little gruff with her."

I raised an eyebrow but remained silent. After a moment, Reyes added, "Yeah, I was too hard on her. Winston hollered at me about it last night, too, and for good reason. I'll go out there and apologize."

Reyes stood, pulled his wallet out of his back pocket, and began to count out cash. As I watched, I remembered Mama's advice to me after Damien had stormed out of the séance. I touched Reyes lightly on the shoulder. "Wait, please," I said. "She might need to calm down a bit before she's ready to hear your apology."

Reyes looked at me, then toward the door, then back at me. With a sigh, he tucked the cash into a front pocket, put away his wallet, and sat down again. "You're probably right. I'll drive out to the farm this afternoon. Maybe I'll take along a little something from the bakery."

"You can't go wrong with the cinnamon rolls."

Reyes gave me a sad smile. "I really was just trying to do my job."

"Of course you were. But Winston and Kenzie both had a lot to deal with last night. Even before everything that happened, I'm sure they were both stressed about getting the festival started on the right foot. As for Winston's behavior just now, remember, someone died on his property last night. I'm sure it's bringing up some strong emotions, and probably a bit of fear for him. The way he yelled at you isn't really about you."

Even as I said that, I thought of Winston's sly smile the night before as he'd told Damien how good he expected business to be. Everyone would want their chance to wander the murder maze, wondering when they were in the exact spot where Annabelle had died.

"You're right," Reyes said, interrupting my thoughts. He silently gazed at me for so long I started to squirm on my stool. Even without saying a word, the man was making me feel like I was being interrogated. Finally, his face softened. "You're surprisingly insightful, Olivia."

Oh, good, he's back to using my first name.

"I've been through a lot in the last year or so," I told him. "It's made me much better at seeing past the facades people put up." I laughed suddenly. "Someday, you and I should grab a beer at the saloon. For as often as we wind up face to face, we hardly know each other."

"All I know about you is that you're the reason I have to drive halfway to Tucson now to consult with a psychic. Oh, and I know that you always wind up in the middle of my murder investigations."

"Except," I said, raising a finger, "this time around, it's not a murder investigation."

Reyes turned and looked toward the front door again. "I wonder," he said quietly.

CHAPTER TWELVE

I didn't respond to Reyes's comment. The idea that Annabelle had been murdered seemed a lot more likely than her having a very unexpected cardiac event. Didn't Reyes realize how many people in Nightmare disliked her?

Then again, there were all those men coming through the haunt who had been more interested in her than the fun frights they had paid money for. Even I had to concede that there was, in fact, an Annabelle bandwagon, and plenty of people were on it.

Reyes threw his napkin on top of the remains of his lunch and pushed the plate away from him. He plunked the cash he had taken out earlier onto the counter and stood. "I've got work to do," he mumbled, more to himself than to me.

I waved goodbye, but Reyes already had his back to me. *Good. Maybe he'll do some more digging and find signs that this was a murder.*

"That was a weird scene, right?" Ella asked.

I turned to see her slowly collecting the cash and the plate. "You mean Kenzie sobbing and Winston yelling? Yeah, it was weird."

Ella put the plate down and leaned over the counter toward me. "Officer Reyes is really well respected in this town. I've never seen anyone yell at him like that. He's a good cop."

"I'm sure you're right, but when people feel like they're being accused of something they didn't do, it can cause some strong reactions." I gave Ella a knowing look, and she laughed self-consciously.

"I know, I know. I've been on the receiving end of his interrogations, but I didn't yell." Ella stared into space for a moment, then added, "I did cry a bit, though. Okay, I cried a lot."

"You also knew you hadn't murdered anyone," I said thoughtfully. "Maybe Kenzie or Winston has something to hide."

"Maybe they both have something to hide. By the way, was your cheeseburger okay?"

I gestured toward my empty plate. "Obviously. Why wouldn't it be?"

"Our day cook is out because of what happened at the fall festival."

I tilted my head and peered at Ella. "Oh?"

"Hal and Annabelle had a little thing going last year, when she was here for the Halloween season. He's so broken up about her death that he called out today."

"A little thing," I repeated. "Let me guess: this is the guy who Annabelle nearly killed last year? Mama didn't know the details, but she said you might."

Ella laughed, her gold hoop earrings swinging with the movement. "Of course you've already heard about that incident. I overheard Reyes saying he suspected you were already investigating, and he was right! But I wouldn't say Annabelle almost killed him. It's more that he nearly died trying to please her."

"First of all," I said, "I'm not investigating anything. I'm just trying to find out what happened since she was in earshot of me when she died."

"Sounds like investigating to me."

"Well… Okay, so maybe I am. Reyes isn't convinced it was murder, but I am, so I'm doing what I can to help." At least, that was what I was telling myself. It was also possible that I was simply nosy and couldn't help but dive into something that had nothing to do with me. "So what happened with the cook?"

"It's too long to tell during the lunch rush. You want some pie while you wait for things to quiet down?"

Clues *and* pie? I quickly agreed, and soon, I was enjoying a slice of pecan pie with a big dollop of whipped cream on top of it. I savored each bite, knowing it would be a while yet before the lunch crowd wrapped up and headed back to their offices and shops. Or, in the case of the woman near me who was wearing a long calico dress and had her hair twisted up into a bun, back to pretending to be a Nightmare resident from the eighteen hundreds.

By the time I took my last bite of pie, there were only two of us remaining at the counter. I thought the man would never finish his bowl of chili, but finally, he paid and left, and Ella came over to me, leaned her elbows on the counter, and began, "Annabelle showed up around this time last year to help out at the Sanctuary. Every single guy in this town started falling all over themselves for her. She went to the saloon every night, and from what I hear, she never paid for her own drinks, because there were guys practically fighting each other for the honor."

I was slightly surprised Annabelle had chosen to spend her evenings at the Nightmare Saloon rather than at Under the Undertaker's. Either she preferred humans to supernatural creatures, or she had figured her chances of getting someone else to buy her drinks was better at the saloon.

"So, Hal, he goes down to the saloon one night, and he meets her," Ella continued. "They start this little

Halloween fling. I mean, everyone knew she wasn't going to stay in Nightmare past the end of October, but Hal was acting like he'd found the woman he wanted to spend the rest of his life with. He was obsessed."

"Annabelle seemed to have that effect on people," I noted. It must have been that ethereal glow Damien had told me about. "But how did he wind up close to death because of her?"

Ella looked around, like she didn't want anyone to overhear us. "Apparently, she told Hal that if he really liked her, then he needed to prove it. There was some diamond bracelet or something she had seen in the window of Jordan Jewelers, over in the New Downtown area. She told Hal she wanted it, but Hal said he couldn't afford it. So, Annabelle told him to figure out another way to get it for her."

"Oh, no." I groaned, guessing what was coming next. "He stole it for her, didn't he?"

"He tried, but Hal isn't a criminal. He went into the store, grabbed the jewelry, and made a run for it. Stupid, stupid move! Mr. Jordan was standing right there, and all he had to do was throw out an arm. Hal went flying, right into a glass display case."

I hissed in my breath. "Ouch."

"He nearly died from blood loss. I forget how many stitches he got, but it was over two dozen. He also got arrested, though Mr. Jordan worked out a deal with Hal. He had to pay for the broken display case and the cleanup, and he had to volunteer out at the old cemetery to help clear out all the weeds." Ella shook her head. "All for some girl he'd just met."

"Annabelle asked him to steal, but Hal's near-death accident is all his fault. You're right, it was a stupid thing to do. How did Annabelle react to his failed attempt to get the jewelry?"

"Hal said she was still demanding the bracelet, so he started forking over all his extra cash so she could eventually buy it herself. She showed up at the saloon wearing it one night, but Hal hadn't given her nearly enough to afford it since he was also paying back Mr. Jordan."

"She probably got her other admirers to chip in." I shook my head. I didn't know Hal, but I felt sorry for him. It sounded like he had fallen under Annabelle's spell, similar to what I had seen from guests coming through the Sanctuary on Wednesday night. "I hope Hal ended things with her after that."

"Nope. He never stopped thinking she was the most incredible woman in the world."

"No wonder he's too upset to work today. At least he wasn't on the scene last night, like I was."

"Oh, he was there. The Lusty does a pop-up grill at the festival every year, and Hal was working it last night. I assume he saw Annabelle there before she died, but I haven't talked to him since everything went down."

"Hmm." I was too busy thinking to give any other kind of response. Surely Hal had known Annabelle was back in Nightmare, and I doubted he would have wasted a moment in tracking her down at the festival. Had Hal been the one making Annabelle giggle just before she died? Maybe she had been flirting with him, trying to get him to pull some new crazy stunt for her.

"Since we're not busy right now," Ella began, looking at me slyly, "want to see the shrine?"

"Shrine?"

"Come around." Ella gestured for me to walk behind the counter, into the area where the servers came and went from the doors to the kitchen. I had been in the kitchen before, in the aftermath of a dishwasher dying face-down in one of the sinks there, but I hadn't explored the area.

Ella led me through the swinging double doors, past

the door to the manager's office, and around the corner. We cruised past the cooktop, then Ella stopped and gestured to the wall above a rack of bowls. "There," she said.

It really was a shrine. Hal had taped photos of Annabelle to the wall. He was with her in some of the shots, while others had clearly been trimmed to cut out other people. Annabelle was looking at the camera in some photos, but most were candid, like Hal had taken them when she wasn't looking. The photos gave me all kinds of stalker vibes.

There was a white napkin pinned to the wall with a thumbtack. The napkin had writing on it, with what appeared to be a line from a pop song about falling in love. There was also a menu for a restaurant and a dried flower pinned in place.

"This is a bit…disconcerting." I frowned at the sea of smiling Annabelles in front of me. Did I need to add Hal to my suspect list? If he was that obsessed with Annabelle, then who knew what he might have done if she had rejected his advances on her return to Nightmare, or if he had caught her flirting with someone else. Maybe it had been another man making her giggle, and Hal had found them there in the maze.

"Is he a nice guy?" I asked suddenly.

"Hal? Sure, he's a decent human being, except when it came to this lady. We've been begging him since last November to take down the photos, but he flat refuses."

"People do strange things for love."

"Yeah. And it seems like Annabelle was awfully young to just drop dead all by herself."

"You're not the first to say so."

Neither Ella nor I spoke as we both walked back into the dining area. I didn't think she had really considered Annabelle's death might have been murder, or that her friend and co-worker might have had something to do with it, until that moment. Showing me the shrine had been a bit of a lark, but suddenly, it felt deadly serious.

"Thanks for the tour," I told her. "I'm going to head on out."

"Oh, and if this is a murder, and you do investigate it," Ella said, stopping me from going with a hand on my shoulder, "you should ask that woman who ran out of here crying what she knows."

"Kenzie? Winston's assistant manager at the festival? I think Reyes already wrung all the details out of her."

Ella's mouth twisted into something like a sinister smile. "I doubt she mentioned that she was dating Hal right up until Annabelle showed up last year."

CHAPTER THIRTEEN

"And why," I said, crossing my arms and trying—but failing—to frown at Ella, "didn't you give me that little tidbit earlier?"

"Honestly, I hadn't thought much about Hal and his relationship with Annabelle until you started hinting about murder." Ella smiled sweetly and made a face of mock innocence. "Plus, maybe I was waiting for the right moment to drop that bombshell. It was pretty fun to see your expression!"

"If they had been dating, then surely Reyes already knows," I said. "Nightmare isn't a big town."

Ella gave a little shrug. "He's got better things to do than worry about who's dating who. Besides, it was a year ago that Hal and Kenzie broke up. Seriously, you should chat with Kenzie. I don't really know her, so I can't say whether she's the killer type, but you might learn something."

"I think I'll let her calm down before I try." I thanked Ella for the tip and left. During my walk back to Cowboy's Corral, I had a lot to sift through in my mind. Callie and Kenzie both had former boyfriends who had abandoned them for Annabelle. Winston had been publicly embarrassed by her so badly that he had threatened to cut ties with the Sanctuary. Hal might have loved her so much that he killed her out of jealousy, and Daniel might have killed her because she stole a job out from under him when he had desperately needed the money.

For something that was, according to Reyes, not a murder, there sure were a lot of suspects. Even Felipe had reason to dislike Annabelle, though I didn't think "the chupacabra did it" was the kind of logic that would hold up in a murder case.

I had gotten most of my work done for the motel that morning, but once I got back to my apartment, I was too restless to relax. So, I grabbed my laptop and went back to the front office, hoping I could distract myself with some marketing work. I would make up something to do, if it came down to it.

As soon as I walked through the office door, Mama said, "Your brain is buzzing, and you need to get your thoughts under control."

I stopped walking and stared at Mama, my mouth agape. "Wow, how can you tell?"

"I just know." Mama smiled proudly at me, then chuckled. "Also, the laptop cord is dragging behind you like a leash without a dog attached. You're clearly distracted." She pointed, and I saw that the cord trailed all the way out onto the sidewalk in front of the office. The door had closed on it, so I had to open it a crack to retrieve the cord.

"It's kind of your fault I'm distracted," I said with a sly smile. "You're the one who told me to go talk to Ella." I filled Mama in on the story of Hal's obsession with Annabelle and his disastrous attempt at robbery. She just shook her head and rolled her eyes.

"You did enough work for me this morning," Mama said after I had finished the tale. "What you need to do is sit down and conjure up a resolution to Annabelle's death. We want to know, for absolute certain, if this was a murder or not. And if it was a murder, then we want to know who did it. I'll stay quiet while you conjure." Mama pointed to a chair, and I sat in it dutifully.

I wiggled my rear end as I sank down into the chair and found a cozy position. Once I had, I leaned my head against the high back of the chair and closed my eyes. I thought, over and over again, how much I wanted to know exactly what had transpired in Annabelle's death.

I sat there in deep concentration until the bell over the door announced someone's arrival. I cracked one eye open and saw a man walking to the desk, and I overheard him asking about the room rate. After Mama got him squared away, I tried to settle back into conjuring mode, but my brain had started to think about other things, and I had a hard time reining it in.

Damien called while I was giving myself a mental lecture about needing to focus. When I answered, he said, "I need to borrow you for a bit before you go to work tonight. I'll pick you up at five thirty."

"Okay." I was about to ask what we would be doing, but Damien had hung up. "Well," I said to my phone.

After that, I was definitely too distracted to continue my conjuring practice. Instead, I went back to my apartment and gave the place a thorough dusting. I opened the windows, too, to air out the tiny studio. I had a feeling the orange shag carpet needed a deep clean, but I would save that for a later date.

I had no idea what Damien needed to "borrow" me for, which meant I had no idea what I was supposed to wear. Were we going somewhere that required a nicer look, like a Chamber of Commerce mixer? Would my Sanctuary T-shirt be sufficient?

In the end, I opted for black slacks and a royal-blue blouse that hugged my curves nicely. I stuffed my Sanctuary T-shirt into my purse, so I could swap my top once I got to work that night.

Halfway through brushing out my auburn hair, I stopped and stared at myself in the mirror. I hadn't gotten my hair cut since moving to Nightmare. In fact, I had been overdue for an appointment even before leaving Nashville. Since I had been broke, letting my hair grow out hadn't really been a choice but a necessity.

I raised a hand and ran my fingers through the ends, which were slightly below my shoulders. I kind of liked the softer look of longer hair. It fit the softer me, who wasn't always stressed out about work and pulling long hours.

I had moved on from my hair to my lipstick when there was a knock at my door. In the past, when Damien had picked me up for something, he had typically waited in his car for me. According to my watch, I still had two minutes, so he certainly hadn't bothered to come up the stairs because I was late.

When I opened the door, all I could see at first was a big bouquet of lilies and baby's breath. I started to gasp, but my throat closed up. I couldn't make a sound.

Is this a date? I thought. My mind immediately went back to that moment in Damien's office, when our faces had been so very close together, and he had started to say something but never got to finish it. Had Damien decided to take a chance and take me out?

"Time to do the polite thing," Damien said flatly.

I blinked at him several times, both confused and still trying to get my throat to cooperate. The only thing I could muster was an ungraceful, "Huh?"

"You know how this town is. Someone already started a memorial to Annabelle."

"Of course they did," I said. Now that I knew the flowers weren't for me, I had sufficiently recovered to speak in actual words. "And it's important to show that the Sanctuary is a part of this town, and their grief is our grief."

"Exactly. The normal people of Nightmare already

judge us, and if we don't show up, that will only deepen the divide." Damien looked at the flowers. "They were expensive, but I think they're a tax write-off since Annabelle was an employee."

A feeling of sadness suddenly welled up in me. "That poor girl," I said. "I wonder if she had any idea how many of us didn't care for her."

"I doubt she did. There were enough people telling her how wonderful she was, and she clearly didn't feel the need to change her behavior."

I left the front door open as I grabbed my purse from the small round table that served as both my desk and the dining room table. "It must be nice to have even one person tell you how wonderful you are," I said wistfully.

Damien handed the flowers to me as we walked down the stairs to the motel parking lot. He had left his silver Corvette parked right at the foot of the stairs, and he opened the door for me so I could slide into the passenger seat. I carefully balanced the flowers on my lap and buckled up as he came around to the other side.

Soon, we were on our way to Byers Farm. The kickoff party had been a nighttime event, but following that, the Nightmare Fall Festival was open during the day, too. When we arrived, the cow pasture was packed with cars, and families were streaming toward the cluster of pavilions.

Damien and I parked and joined the throng. I noticed a young man carrying a bouquet, too, and I asked Damien, "How did you hear about the memorial?"

"Winston called and told me about it. Three other people called to tell me the news after that. Clearly, the memorial is some of the top gossip in Nightmare."

We made a beeline for the maze entrance, and over the heads and shoulders of the people in front of us, we could see shiny silver balloons floating above the cornstalks. They swayed slowly in the late-afternoon sky. When we got closer, I stopped and whispered, "Wow."

I had seen plenty of makeshift memorials, most recently in Nightmare following Kelly Lowry's murder. The memorial to Annabelle made them all pale in comparison. There was an easel set up with a huge photo of Annabelle on it, smiling and stretching her arms wide underneath a Nightmare Fall Festival banner. Around it were dozens of bouquets, candles, several Teddy bears, and quite a few handwritten notes.

A large, printed sign had been hung from the cornstalk above the memorial. *Gone but not forgotten. Annabelle Yates, you will always live in our hearts.*

Damien leaned down and said into my ear, "What was that you were saying about her being a poor girl?"

"She had a lot of admirers," I admitted. Even as I said that, though, I thought again of what Winston had said about Annabelle's death being a way to bring in business. He had probably been the one who printed and hung the sign, and if I had to guess, I would have said he placed the first bouquet to get things started. The more people were reminded of what had happened in the maze, the more they would want to pay the extra money to go inside it.

"Let's get this over with." Damien straightened up and gently plucked the bouquet out of my hand.

Just as Damien took his first step toward the memorial, though, someone shoved their way past him. Damien stumbled and knocked into me, and I instinctively grabbed his arm to steady him.

Once I was sure Damien wasn't going to fall over, I looked to see who had smacked into him. It was a man with shaggy, dirty-blond hair. His plaid flannel shirt flapped with the speed of his running.

As I watched, the man came to an abrupt stop and threw himself down onto his knees in front of the memorial. He clutched the sides of his head, looked up at the sky, and wailed, "Annabelle!"

I still had a grip on Damien's arm, and I leaned closer to him and whispered, "Looks like we're not the only ones trying to make a show of our grief."

CHAPTER FOURTEEN

Someone else ran past us. "Hal! Hal, hey, come on." I recognized Jeff, the manager of The Lusty Lunch Counter. He kneeled down next to Hal and put an arm around his shoulders. Hal didn't respond; he just wailed loudly.

"So that's Hal," I said under my breath. When Ella had said Hal was obsessed with Annabelle, she hadn't been kidding. It was one thing to be upset about a loved one's death, but what Hal was doing was a little extreme. I felt horrible for him, but at the same time, it seemed a little like he was putting on a show.

"Hal and Annabelle had a thing when she was in Nightmare last year," I whispered to Damien. "He's got a wall of photos of her up next to his cooktop at The Lusty. He was dating Kenzie, the assistant manager here, before Annabelle showed up and stole him away, so Kenzie is someone we need to keep an eye on."

Damien snorted, and his hand shot up to cover his mouth. His shoulders shook, and I heard a muffled laugh. After a moment, he lowered his hand and said, "Of course you're tracking down suspects already!"

"Why is that funny?" I asked, frowning.

"Because you're so predictable."

"I'm just trying to get some closure in all this. Since the police aren't treating it as a murder, I am."

Damien snorted out a laugh again. "Stop making me laugh, Olivia. Cracking up at the memorial is only going to make *me* look guilty of murder."

I failed to see the humor in wanting to know the truth. In a defensive tone, I said, "I'm treating my investigation as a conjuring exercise, of course. If I can hone my skills enough to find a killer, then maybe I can learn to use them well enough to help find your dad."

That sobered Damien right up. "You're right," he said tightly. "You're clearly doing a better job of looking for my father than I am."

"What? Damien, that's not what I meant."

"It's true, though."

I had let go of Damien's arm, but I grabbed it again. To make sure he was paying attention to me, I spun to face him, looking up at him defiantly. "I know you want to find Baxter even more than I do, but I also know you've got a much bigger barrier to exploring your abilities. I didn't believe I was supernatural at all, but your dad made you believe that your supernatural power is dangerous, and that you can't trust yourself. I can't imagine how hard that is, Damien, but I believe in you. I trust you."

One corner of Damien's mouth twitched. "But you don't even know what I'm capable of."

"And we never will unless you start exploring your abilities. You pretend not to care about the Sanctuary or the people in it, but I see how protective you are of them. I know you care more than you let on, and I also know you'll be very careful to control your abilities so you don't hurt anyone."

Even in the daylight, I could see the way Damien's eyes were glowing softly. I suddenly worried I had said too much, and that I had made him angry. I slowly uncurled my fingers from around his arm and took a step back.

Damien took one step forward. He was still staring at me intently when I heard a sniffle to my left.

I looked over and saw Jeff leading Hal away from the memorial. As Jeff passed us, he glanced at me and gave me a look that clearly said, *Can you believe this?*

By the time I looked at Damien again, his attention was focused on the memorial. He sighed. "Let's do this."

Together, we walked forward and stood solemnly in front of the pile of flowers and candles. After the conversation we'd just had, it was easy to look forlorn. When Damien seemed satisfied that we had stood there long enough, he leaned down and laid the flowers at the front of the pile.

We turned to leave, and I saw just how much the crowd in front of the maze had grown. Damien had wanted to publicly show that the Sanctuary was feeling Annabelle's loss, and we had certainly had a sizable audience for our public display of grief.

Neither one of us said a word until we had moved past the crowd. I suggested stopping by the Sanctuary's booth to see how Daniel and Sam were doing, but Damien wanted to find Winston first.

It wasn't hard to spot him. He was wearing a pumpkin-orange shirt and walking from one pavilion to the next, and I swear, he had a bounce in his step.

We caught up to Winston as he was on his way toward the pumpkin patch, and he grinned when he saw us. "Out here to pay your respects, are you?"

"Of course," Damien said.

"You're not the only ones! Look at this crowd!" Winston gestured grandly at the people streaming past us. "This is the best Friday attendance I've ever had, and it's not even dark yet! I might have to open an overflow parking lot in the old alfalfa field!"

I glanced at Damien out of the corner of my eye, and I

could see the slightly horrified look on his face. I was sure I had a similar expression. With effort, I said, "I'm so happy business is good. I hope everyone has a fun time."

"This festival is what keeps my farm up and running. I won't be losing any sleep this next year. Yes, business is very good." Winston took another satisfied look around, then hurried off.

Damien looked at me wryly. "Please tell me he's on your suspect list, too."

"He hasn't exactly been sad about what happened."

"No. He's too busy mentally counting money. Then again, I've never known Winston to be a particularly sentimental person. He could be a killer, but I think it's more likely just a personality flaw."

"Hal has too much feeling, and Winston doesn't have enough," I commented.

We didn't talk a lot on our drive to the Sanctuary, but it wasn't the unpleasant, awkward kind of silence I'd endured with Damien before. I could tell we were both deep in thought, and I was content to stare out the window at the deep pink clouds on the edge of the sunset.

Zach was standing in front of the ticket window when we arrived, hanging a sign about a discount for anyone with a Fall Festival ticket stub, and he turned and gazed at us with a smirk as we approached the front doors.

Damien kept walking, saying he was going to his office, but I wandered over to Zach. "What?" I asked.

Zach's dark-brown eyes were sparkling with humor. "You two arrived together. Something I should know about?"

I wanted to roll my eyes and protest that whatever Zach was implying, he was wrong. At the same time, I knew that was exactly the reaction he wanted. Instead, I looked at him gravely. "We went to the festival to place flowers at the memorial to Annabelle. Damien thought it was important for the Sanctuary to have a presence there."

"What a boring answer," Zach said. He turned his attention back to the sign, so I headed inside, changed into my Sanctuary T-shirt, and went to the dining room for the night's family meeting.

The meeting felt blessedly normal after the strange events of the past couple of days. It was business as usual as Justine ran through her announcements and assigned roles to those of us who floated around depending on where we were needed.

After the meeting wrapped up, I headed straight for Seraphina. She was leaning over the side of her small water tank on wheels, chatting with Vivian and her girlfriend, Fiona. Seraphina tossed her long golden hair over her shoulder as I approached, and the overhead lights gleamed against her greenish skin.

"Olivia, you look like most of us do on November first," Seraphina said, peering at me. "You need sleep."

"I need people to stop getting murdered," I commented.

Fiona laughed, a rich, deep sound. "Now you know what it's like to be me! Always someone dying." As a banshee, Fiona's whole life had been filled with death, but she was a lot better at handling it than I was.

"You're a siren," I said to Seraphina, "so it makes sense to me that men lose their minds over you. But what about fairies? Do they have the ability to lure men, too?"

"Is this about Annabelle? I noticed last year how guys were constantly falling all over themselves for her." I could hear the distaste in Seraphina's voice. When I nodded, she continued, "It's not just sirens who can be charming. Even humans can be enticing. Unfortunately, I understand Annabelle was both enticing and manipulative. Not all fairies are good ones, like Clara."

"I am very, very good," Clara piped up. She had been walking past and overheard us. "And Sera is right, Olivia. Fairies aren't always nice, just like people aren't always nice. I mean, look at Damien."

Clara was obviously fighting to keep from smiling as she looked at me with raised eyebrows. She was trying to get me to pipe up in defense of Damien, I was sure. Instead, what I said was, "No comment."

I was surprised, then, when Vivian came to Damien's defense. "He's dealing with a lot right now. The poor guy just found out his mother still exists somewhere in the ether, and she won't even show up to talk to him. It doesn't give him the right to be a jerk, but it does explain it."

"Aw, you're no fun," Clara said. "But, since I'm a good fairy, I won't hold it against you."

Vivian smiled slyly. "If you did, I'd make sure your next palm reading foresaw terrible things in your future."

"Speaking of foresight," Clara said, "I was right to warn Callie about what she said in front of you. Now, she's worried that she's suspect number one in Annabelle's murder."

"According to the police, it wasn't murder." I turned to Fiona. "Did you know Annabelle was going to die? Did you get that banshee flash of insight?"

"No. But then, I hadn't interacted with her much, and she died miles from here. I don't get the flash for everyone."

"Besides," Clara said, "I don't care what the police think, and neither does Callie. Just in case this was a murder, Callie wants to make sure her name is nowhere near your suspect list. She's upstairs, in my apartment, waiting to tell you everything she knows."

CHAPTER FIFTEEN

"I'm in the lagoon vignette tonight," I told Clara apologetically. "I've got to get into my costume, so I won't be able to talk to Callie until after we close."

Clara waved a hand. "Oh, she knows that. She wanted to talk to you, but she also wanted to hide out a bit, I think. She took the night off work, and she's upstairs binging a reality show. She'll be just fine until we wrap things up at midnight."

I was looking forward to being in the lagoon vignette after spending the past several nights either taking tickets or standing uncomfortably in a maze. I would be able to frighten people without being frightened myself, and the huge crowds would give me plenty of chances to do just that.

At the same time, though, I was anxious to hear whatever Callie had in store for me.

Before long, I was decked out in my usual pirate costume, which consisted of a long red coat and a matching skirt, plus a black shirt with lace at the cuffs. My hair was tucked up inside a tricorn hat, and I had amped up my makeup to look more dramatic. I resisted the urge to check on Damien, especially since we opened in just ten minutes, and headed straight for the lagoon vignette.

Theo and Seraphina were already there when I

entered through the hidden door that led to a network of passages that linked all the scenes of the haunted house. Seraphina was swimming a somersault in her big glass-sided tank, her silver tail flashing. Beside the tank, the prop pirate ship loomed up, looking ominous in the dim lighting of the room.

The lagoon scene had some shallow pools of water in it, and guests walked on a wooden boardwalk so they would feel like they were traversing an actual lagoon. I always stood near the door that led to the next scene, so I could hurry along any stragglers.

No sooner had I taken up my usual spot than Theo stalked up to me. He grinned, which always looked sinister when he had his zombie makeup on. "Do I have to protect you from a dangerous criminal tonight? Any murder suspects I need to keep an eye out for?"

"Those things don't happen that often," I pointed out. "And the answer to both questions is no."

Theo swept off his pirate hat and bowed low. "A pity. I always enjoy getting to play the hero. Please be sure to find someone suspicious soon, so I can swoop into action."

The overhead lights blinked three times just then, indicating the Sanctuary was open for business, and the first guests of the night were being let in, so I said, "Right now, the most heroic thing you can do is get one of the first ten people to scream."

"It will be one of the first five," Theo promised.

Theo was true to his word. In fact, from my vantage point, the screamer appeared to be the second person in the first group of guests who came into the lagoon. Theo followed them all the way to where I was standing, and after they had hustled out of the scene, shrieking and giggling, he looked at me. "Now, I challenge you to do the same with the next group!"

Our little game continued right up until Justine

arrived to give me my break. I couldn't believe it was already time to grab a snack. I was having so much fun with Theo that I hadn't thought about Callie a single time. I hadn't thought about Annabelle either, for that matter.

Mori and I usually had the same break time, and she glided into the dining room right on my heels. Felipe typically stayed upstairs, in Mori's apartment, while the Sanctuary was open, but on this night, he was with her. "Does he have fun scaring people?" I asked.

"He's helping Fiona in the cemetery vignette, and he loves it." Mori reached down and patted Felipe's head. "He runs around the prop headstones, and between the shadows and the fog machines, people only get a glimpse of him. By the time they get to the corridor I haunt, half of them say they're seeing things, and the other half claim it must be a mechanical dog prop!"

"Except mechanical dogs don't get treats!" I went to the snack table and grabbed my usual bag of potato chips and package of chocolate-chip cookies. Felipe was always happy to help clean up any crumbs I happened to drop.

I settled onto a bench with Mori and Felipe, where I munched on my snack happily while we chatted. Eventually, the conversation turned to Annabelle.

"I asked Seraphina if fairies could lure men, like sirens," I said. "I also wondered if she could mesmerize, like you vampires do."

"I think Annabelle was the fairy version of the most popular girl in school," Mori said with a sigh. "Not that I went to school. Back in my day, girls of my economic status were taught how to embroider panels, play the harpsichord, and be good wives. But I've seen plenty of movies about popular girls."

I tried to picture Mori, sitting on a couch in an oversized T-shirt and pajama pants while eating ice cream right out of the carton and watching a teen angst movie. The mental image just didn't work for me.

"She was charismatic," I agreed. "And she knew the right things to say, and the right way to act, to get what she wanted." I thought of poor Hal, who had been foolish enough to attempt robbery for her. No supernatural power had prompted him to do that. It had simply been obsessive infatuation.

Maybe love is more dangerous than supernatural power.

Mori laughed, snapping me out of my dark thoughts. "How have you had time to think about Annabelle with these crowds tonight? Weekends in October are exhausting. I'm going to be fast asleep long before sunrise!"

"I wasn't thinking about it until I stopped scaring people to go on break." I checked my watch. "I promise I'll put it out of my mind in six minutes and thirty-seven seconds."

I finished my snack and, just as I had promised Mori, I returned to the lagoon vignette and lost myself in scaring guests once again.

Usually, as the clock ticked closer to midnight, the stream of people coming through the haunt would dwindle. With Halloween just around the corner, though, the guests kept coming, until I spotted Malcolm walking slowly behind a group. "Just keeping an eye out for stragglers," he said as he passed me.

Not long after that, the overhead lights blared to life again, which meant the final group had exited the old hospital building. I hollered a quick good night to Theo and Seraphina, then hustled to the costume room so I could change back into my T-shirt and jeans. I didn't even bother to take off my makeup before I went in search of Clara and Callie.

I found Clara in the entryway, chatting with Justine and Zach. "You ready?" she asked as soon as she saw me.

"Lead the way!"

"Wait," Zach said, raising an arm to block my path. "Don't you need to kiss Damien good night first?"

"Not part of my job description," I said, sidestepping his arm to follow Clara up the sweeping staircase.

Why is Zach teasing me like this? I walked up the stairs slowly, wondering if Damien or I had said something Zach had taken the wrong way.

And then it hit me. It wasn't something we had said. It was something we had done. Zach *had* observed just how closely Damien had been standing to me in his office that day, and he had clearly made some inferences. I could feel my cheeks burning, and I made sure to keep my head turned so Zach wouldn't spot my embarrassment.

Clara glanced back at me when we reached the second floor. "You okay?"

I gave myself a shake. "Yeah. My brain was elsewhere. Sorry."

Clara didn't say anything, but the knowing look she gave me made my cheeks flush again. *Does she know? Did Zach tell her what he saw?*

Earlier, I had tried to put my talk with Callie out of my mind so the night would go faster. At the moment, I focused on it with all my might to push the other thoughts out of my brain.

We turned left at the second hallway we came to. Clara's apartment was at the far end of it, in the northwest corner of the building. The old hospital rooms had been renovated into apartments, and Clara's place matched her personality. It was bright, with pastel hues and lush throw rugs. Strings of white lights crisscrossed the ceiling of the living room, giving the place a cozy glow.

Callie was sitting on the pale-yellow sofa, her legs tucked up under her. She had a candy bar in one hand and a steaming mug in the other. On the TV, two reality show stars were arguing about something.

"Olivia, thank you so much for meeting with me," Callie said as I walked in. She put down the mug, turned off the TV, then downed her candy bar in three big bites.

"Of course," I said, sitting down next to her. Clara disappeared through a door, and I heard the distinct sound of cabinets being opened and closed. By the time Callie had finished chewing her last bite of candy bar, Clara had returned with a tray. There were three glasses of water on it, plus a bowl filled with gummy bears.

"You fairies like your sweets," I commented as I helped myself.

Clara pointed at my handful of colorful bears. "Maybe you're part fairy!" She sat down cross-legged on the rug in front of the sofa. "Okay, Callie, let's hear your story."

"There's not a lot to tell, really," Callie began. "But if Annabelle was murdered, then I don't want you to think I meant it when I said I hoped she dropped dead."

"I used a similar phrase about my ex-husband during our divorce," I assured her. "I know you didn't really mean it."

Callie picked up a gummy bear and squeezed it between her forefinger and thumb. "I hated growing up in Nightmare. All I ever wanted to do was get out of this tiny little backwater town. So, I applied to Arizona State University, thinking the big city of Phoenix would be everything Nightmare wasn't."

Clara made a gagging noise. "Too many people."

"I loved it," Callie continued. "During my second semester, I met Lance, and we just clicked. By Christmas of my sophomore year, we were starting to talk about what our life after graduation would look like. I was willing to live anywhere that wasn't Nightmare, and Lance was my ticket to a bigger, better life." Callie squeezed the gummy bear harder, then popped it into her mouth.

"Mom and Dad would have flipped if Callie married a non-fairy," Clara said. "But I could see how happy Lance made her, so I hoped it would work out for the two of them."

"Except it didn't," Callie said bitterly. "We were at a house party in January of my sophomore year, and I knew a fairy was there two seconds after we walked inside. I could smell her."

"But you couldn't have known then that she was so…" I searched for the right word.

"No, I didn't, but I saw the way she looked at Lance when they met. And honestly, I think she stole him away from me only because I'm a fairy, too. I think she wanted to prove she was better than me. By the end of the spring semester, Lance had dumped me and was attached at the hip to that monster. I was so heartbroken that I quit school and came back here."

"Callie," I asked gently, "why were you at the festival the night Annabelle died?"

"Because I decided I wanted to see her. I needed to prove to myself that I could see her and not fall apart. I needed to prove that I was stronger than she was. But she was dead before I could do that."

I was about to respond when there was a knock at the door. Clara got up off the floor in one smooth motion to answer it, and soon, Malcolm was walking in. With his black coat and top hat, he looked comically out of place among the pastels and soft lights.

"Hello, ladies. We're having a drink downstairs, if you'd like to join us."

Callie frowned. "Are you toasting to Annabelle's memory?"

"No. We're toasting to a great night of scaring a lot of guests."

"I'm in," Callie said, nodding. "I could use a drink."

We followed Malcolm out the door and down the hallway. As we walked, I told Callie, "I'm so sorry you had to go through that. But, you know, you can do anything you want, or go anywhere you want. You don't need a man to get you out of Nightmare."

"That's the thing. Now that I'm older, I really love this town. I had thought I wanted to escape Nightmare, but I think that's because I hadn't found my place here yet."

Malcolm half-turned so he could look at Callie. "I understand that. It took a long time to find my place here at the Sanctuary, and it transformed me."

"What were you doing before you came here?" I asked.

Malcolm glanced at me, then looked forward again, his face nearly hidden from my view. "You've caught some killers since you came here, Olivia, and you've met some real monsters. There was a time, though, before I met Baxter, when I was the worst thing in the Arizona Territory."

CHAPTER SIXTEEN

"Arizona Territory?" Callie repeated. "Arizona has been a state for more than a century, so just how old are you, Malcolm?"

"Old," Malcolm answered.

Malcolm had hinted at his past before, and how dangerous he had been before he joined the Sanctuary. Callie wanted to know how old Malcolm was, but I had a more important question.

"What are you?" I asked.

We had reached the staircase, and as Malcolm took the first step down, his fingers tightened around the banister. "I'm not sure you're ready to know."

What could be worse than vampires and werewolves? I wondered. "If you and Baxter are the same kind of super-natural creature, then maybe you can help—"

Just then, I looked down and saw Damien stalking into the entryway from the direction of his office. "Speak of the devil," I muttered.

Damien looked up at me at that moment. "I was hoping you were still here," he called.

I took the last few steps and waited until I was closer to Damien to say, "Does this have to do with Annabelle?"

"No." Damien was wearing his mirrored sunglasses,

and there was a tightness to his mouth that put me on alert.

I glanced toward Malcolm, Clara, and Callie, who were all standing a short distance away. "I'll catch up with all of you later."

As soon as we were alone, I looked at Damien and simply said, "What is it?"

"You're right."

"About?"

"I should take my mother's advice."

I was stunned that Damien had finally given in, but I was also relieved. For one thing, I wouldn't have to hound him about it anymore. More importantly, though, we would finally begin to learn what Damien's supernatural powers were and how they might help us find Baxter.

Telling Damien any of that would be pointless, since it was everything I had been saying to him ever since he had heard his mother's message. Instead, I asked, "When do you want to start training?"

Damien hesitated. "Saturdays are always busy here, especially at this time of year. Maybe we can train on Sunday. Oh, no, that won't work. I told Mama I would have lunch with her. We could squeeze in a quick training between lunch and when we open here, or we can wait until Monday…"

"No," I said, surprised at how firm my voice sounded. "We're going to start right now."

"But—"

"No buts!" I stepped closer to Damien and lowered my voice so a few Sanctuary employees who were walking past wouldn't overhear me. "I know you're scared of your power, but putting this off will only make the anticipation worse. The sooner we train, the sooner you'll feel better."

Damien stared at me silently. At least, I think he was

staring at me. He could have been taking a cat nap behind those sunglasses, and I wouldn't even know it.

"You've made me do after-midnight training before," I noted.

"Fine." Damien nodded curtly. "But not here. At the mine."

I swept my arm toward the entrance. "Let's go."

I heard a whoop above me, and I looked up to see Tanner floating down the staircase. McCrory took a more practical route for a ghost, simply sinking through the staircase and emerging next to me.

"She's going to be mighty glad," Tanner said to Damien. "Missus Shackleford hasn't sent us any more messages, but we can feel her."

"And she's been worried," McCrory added. "Until a little earlier, when she sent us a wave of relief. We figured it meant you were finally going to heed her advice."

Damien looked around the entryway, like he might spot his mother standing in one of the shadowy corners. "She's watching me? Has she been doing that my whole life?"

"That we can't tell you," McCrory said. "But talk to her as you're going about your day. We ghosts like to be remembered."

Something changed in Damien's face. Before, he had looked nervous, on edge. Knowing Lucille was watching over him seemed to encourage him. His mouth relaxed, and his forehead smoothed as he let go of the tension there. He gave me something that was almost a smile. "After you."

"Thanks, boys," I told the ghosts as I led the way to the door. Their message was exactly what Damien had needed to hear, and I expected Lucille had sent that wave of emotion to them in the hope it would be passed on to her son.

Since it was dark out and Damien was driving, he had

to take off his sunglasses before navigating the narrow dirt road that led away from the Sanctuary. I promised myself that, if the opportunity ever presented itself, I would steal them and hide them until he promised to only put them on when he was outside, and it was sunny.

We didn't speak much on the drive, and even once we were standing together inside the mine's living room, we just looked at each other awkwardly for about half a minute.

"I don't know where to start," Damien finally said.

"Me, neither." I paused, thinking back to the exercises Damien had made me do to find out whether I was a conjuror. "Maybe you should clear your mind of distracting thoughts and focus on how much you want to know what you can do."

"I'm not like you, though."

I shrugged. "We have to start somewhere, and settling your mind is a good idea, no matter what. It's been a stressful few days."

Damien sat down on the couch, leaned back, and closed his eyes. I didn't want to sit there and stare at him while he focused, so I took a seat at the dining room table.

If he's practicing, then so should I. I closed my eyes, too, and thought again how much I wished for some resolution in Annabelle's death. *I want to know the truth. I want to know what happened.*

It was getting easier for me to clear out the clutter in my mind and focus on what I most wanted. I wasn't sure how much time had passed before Damien interrupted with, "It's not working."

I opened my eyes and saw him pacing between the couch and the dining room table. I hadn't even heard him get up. "Your mom was a psychic," I said. "What's something that psychics do to get their magic going?"

"Vivian likes to sit quietly and focus, but that's what I was just trying to do."

"You're not necessarily going to succeed after one try," I said impatiently. "As you should know from training me."

"Maybe this is just too much to tackle tonight," Damien growled.

I didn't want Damien to keep making excuses to put off his training, but I also knew better than to keep pushing at that moment. I stood up and began looking around the living room. The place did look a lot better with the new furniture, but it lacked any kind of personal touch.

"You need some framed photos to make this place your own," I commented off-handedly, looking at one of the walls.

"I got rid of all my photos," Damien said.

"Why?" I asked. I was surprised by his answer, but I forced myself to keep my eyes fixed on the bare rock of the wall. Damien was sometimes better at opening up if I wasn't staring him down.

"Because I didn't want to be reminded of what I lost in coming here."

Something hit the wall just to my right and exploded in a shower of white. I jumped back with a yelp and saw a shattered coffee cup on the ground next to me.

I whirled around and glared at Damien. "If you don't want me asking, just say so! You don't have to throw things at me!"

Damien was staring, horrified, at the cup. "I didn't throw it." His eyes were glowing so brightly I felt like an actual physical force hit me when he looked at me.

I took a step back, my shoulders bumping against the wall. Damien's gaze was more than intense. It felt dangerous. *He* felt dangerous.

There was no reason for either of us to say anything,

because I knew we were both thinking the same thing. Damien had thrown the coffee cup with his mind.

His supernatural power was beginning to wake up.

CHAPTER SEVENTEEN

The silence stretched between us, and inside the thick walls of the mine, it was truly silent. There was no sound of the outside world. It was just Damien and me, looking at each other in shock.

Finally, I said, "Maybe you're telekinetic, like Justine."

Damien shook his head slightly. "I think it's more likely tied to deeper psychic phenomena. Remember, my mother was a powerful psychic. I didn't throw that coffee cup consciously. I think the turmoil in my mind manifested as kinetic energy."

"First," I said, trying to lighten the mood, "you might be the only person I've ever heard use the word *turmoil* in conversation. Second, what you're describing *is* telekinesis, albeit subconscious telekinesis. It proves that your mind is powerful, though you're right that it's probably not the extent of your psychic ability. At least this explains why you weren't getting anywhere sitting on the couch."

"How so?"

"You once told me that the first sign of your supernatural ability happened when you were in high school, and you had to defend Zach from a bunch of bullies. Just now, nothing happened until I asked you a question that clearly upset you. Your power surges with your emotions, Damien, and you've been entirely too calm tonight for anything to happen."

"Until now," Damien said. He sighed and ran a hand through his light-brown hair. "After that fight with those guys in high school, my dad taught me how to suppress my emotions. I knew the state of my mind was closely tied to my ability, but I've spent so many years burying that ability. Nothing like this has happened before."

"It's interesting that my conjuring is more effective when I'm calm and focused. Your power seems to be the opposite. If nothing else, we've learned some very valuable information tonight."

"Yeah. We've learned that I was right to be afraid of hurting you. What if I had hit you instead of the wall with that cup?"

"But you didn't." Tentatively, I added, "What triggered it, anyway? You said you lost something in coming here."

Damien's jaw clenched, and he turned away. I thought he was going to ignore my question altogether and, just in case his power surged again, I raised my hands, ready to fend off any more flying objects.

"I was engaged."

It was a good thing Damien wasn't facing me, because my mouth fell open, and I knew my eyes must have looked like they were in danger of popping out of my head. "I had no idea," I said softly.

"No one here does. I had a good job before I came back here, too. A really good job. Some days, I wonder why I gave it all up."

"You came here to run the Sanctuary in your dad's absence, and you came here to help find him." Damien already knew that, of course, but I couldn't help reminding him that his return to Nightmare had been important. "Why didn't your fiancée come here with you? Did her job keep her in… Where did you live, anyway?"

"Flagstaff. I had a gorgeous condo that looked out over…" Damien shook his head and dropped into a chair at the table. Instead of looking at me again, though, he propped his elbows on the table and rested his head in his hands, his face nearly hidden. "It doesn't matter. It's all gone. I put in my notice at work, and I told her why I had to leave. She told me I was stupid for coming back here. We argued, and we broke up, but it didn't matter. She had said enough that I understood she never really loved me. She loved what I had: the big job, the nice condo, the cool car. When I said I was giving everything up, she gave up on me."

I pulled a chair close to Damien's and sat down next to him. "I'm so sorry." I meant it, too. It explained so much about how unbearable Damien had been when he had first arrived in Nightmare. He had been angry and resentful in those early weeks. His story also made me understand why he kept closing himself off from me. He had opened up to someone else, and she had broken his heart. He wasn't ready to trust someone again.

"In Flagstaff, I thought I had the life I had always dreamed of when I was a teenager here," Damien said. He sounded so miserable that I began to rub his back in an effort to soothe him.

"At least you got to keep the car," I said, hoping to make him smile a bit. "When my relationship fell apart, I had to sell mine for the money."

"Do you miss him?"

Do I? I thought for a moment. Mark had once been incredible, but the Mark I had last seen standing in the driveway of our foreclosed house in Nashville? "I miss who he once was," I said sadly. "But that person hasn't existed for a long time."

"People do surprising things. And love really does make us blind."

"It's not just fairies who can break hearts." I thought of Hal and the scene he had made at Annabelle's memorial. "I'm going to find Hal tomorrow and have a chat with him about his relationship with Annabelle."

Damien made a sound that resembled a laugh, and he sat up and turned to me. "I'm pouring out my soul, and you're thinking about murder?"

"I was thinking about love and how much it complicates things."

"Well, you should think about how you want Hal to give you useful information. Conjure his honesty and openness with you. But you're going to have to conjure at home. I don't want to break anything else, so we're calling it a night. I'll drive you back to your place."

It was after two o'clock in the morning by the time I fell into bed, and I probably didn't move a muscle until I heard my phone ringing. I sat up groggily and grabbed my phone. "Hello?" I mumbled.

"Olivia, it's Luis Reyes. We just got the lab results for Ms. Yates. They confirm what we already knew. This was definitely not a murder."

That woke me up better than three cups of coffee could have. "Are you sure?"

"I'm looking at the report, and there were no toxic substances found on or in Ms. Yates's body."

"And she wasn't strangled to death," I said, more to myself than to Reyes.

"No, there are no signs of a physical altercation of any kind." Reyes paused, then said, "She wasn't murdered, Olivia."

"You were right when you said the same thing at the diner."

"And did you listen to me? Or have you still been trying to solve a murder case that doesn't exist?"

"Well…"

"Exactly. The only mystery here is why Ms. Yates had so much colloidal silver in her throat. I know people are into supplements, but talk about overkill."

I gripped my cell phone. "Silver?"

It hadn't been overkill at all. It had been murder. At least, I thought it had been. I knew silver repelled fairies, but could it kill them, as well? If it could, then that meant whoever had killed Annabelle had to have known she was a fairy.

And of all my suspects, that was only Callie and Daniel.

Before I got ahead of myself, though, I asked Reyes, "Is colloidal silver deadly in high quantities?"

"Anything is deadly in high quantities," Reyes answered, "but there wasn't nearly enough in her esophagus to have killed her. It looks like she took a dropperful of it right before she died, but the two incidents aren't related. We checked to see if the silver was laced with poison, but it was clean."

"I see. Thank you for the update, Officer Reyes."

"Oh, just call me Luis. As much as you and I run into each other, we may as well be on a first-name basis."

"I never *want* to see you." I paused. "That came out wrong. I just meant that I only ever see you when there's a murder investigation going on, and I don't hope for that scenario."

"We didn't have this many murders before you showed up in Nightmare. You're lucky I trust Mama, and she trusts you. Otherwise, we would be getting to know each other a lot better."

I got Reyes's meaning loud and clear. If I didn't have an honest, upstanding local like Mama to vouch for me, Reyes would have been questioning me as a suspect in every case.

"I just have bad timing, I suppose," I said.

"Let's hope we don't run into each other for a long time, Olivia."

"Thanks, Luis." I hung up and stared at my phone as I considered what I had just learned. Annabelle likely had been murdered, but the police would never realize it, because they didn't know the supernatural world existed. They would never question a bit of colloidal silver someone had just swallowed, because they didn't know silver was dangerous for some supernatural creatures. As far as the police were concerned, this case was closed.

Which meant it would be up to me—and my friends at the Sanctuary—to track down the truth.

CHAPTER EIGHTEEN

I had told Damien I wanted to speak to Hal about Annabelle, but after what Reyes had relayed, I wasn't sure it was even necessary. If the colloidal silver had been what killed Annabelle, then I was looking for someone who knew about the supernatural world. Hal was likely in the same boat as most of the residents of Nightmare: completely, blissfully unaware that anything like fairies were real.

And, again, that left me with just Daniel and Callie as suspects.

I really, really didn't want it to be Callie. I liked Clara a lot, and the last thing I wanted to do was accuse her sister of murder. Plus, Callie had already given me her side of the story.

It was time to talk to Daniel.

Well, almost. First, though, I had to get out of bed and get ready for the day. I knew that, no matter what was in store, it was going to be a long one. Even if everything was smooth sailing, it was a Saturday in October, which meant work that night was going to be exhausting thanks to the crowds.

I checked the time and saw it was only nine in the morning. Reyes must have called me as soon as he got the lab report. The fall festival opened at ten, and even though

I was tempted to be there the second it was open, I told myself to slow down.

"Pace yourself, Liv," I said as I started my coffee maker.

I showered while the coffee percolated, and I had just sat down at the table with my first cup of the day when there was a knock on my door. I was instantly alert because everyone at the Sanctuary would still be asleep, and Mama rarely showed up unannounced.

When I looked out of the peephole, I could only see a dark mass of curls at the bottom edge of my vision. I instantly opened the door. "Lucy!"

"Hi, Miss Olivia." Mama's granddaughter was smiling up at me, but there was something off about it. Normally, she was a ball of energy, but her stance and her expression were subdued.

"What's wrong?" I asked, leaning down, as if I could figure out the answer if I looked at her closely enough.

"Grandma said I should come talk to you."

"About what?"

Lucy's voice was barely above a whisper. "The dead girl."

I took Lucy's hand and led her inside. "Sit down. You want a mug of hot chocolate?"

Lucy nodded, her curls bobbing around her head, and settled in at the table. As I filled a mug with water and put it in the microwave, I reminded myself to stay calm. Lucy was only ten, and I didn't want to worry her.

"So," I said, forcing myself to sound casual, "this is about Annabelle?"

"Who's Annabelle?"

"The dead girl. The one who died in the corn maze at the fall festival."

"Oh, that." Lucy shrugged, like people dropped dead

in corn mazes all the time. "No, I'm talking about the dead girl on the playground at school."

"Oh." I drew out the word as the truth of what Lucy was saying hit me. She had told me about seeing a "bad-feeling girl" on the playground at school a couple of times, and although I had realized she was describing a ghost, Lucy had thought it was a real person. She had inherited more than her Great-aunt Lucille's name.

"I saw her again this week, during recess. I started walking toward her and"—Lucy banged both palms on the table, my empty coffee cup rattling with the force—"she was just gone. And I thought maybe she wasn't a real person, but a ghost."

"I've had the same thought, based on what you've said about your friends not being able to see her. Plus, she always seemed to disappear when you weren't looking."

"Except this time, I was looking. She has such a mean face, and she feels so bad. If she was a real person, I would know what to do. But, a ghost? A real, actual, spooky, scary ghost?"

The microwave dinged, so I pulled out the mug of water and added the powdered hot chocolate mix. I thought over how I should respond to Lucy as I stirred. By the time I put the mug on the table in front of her and sat down, I felt like I had come up with some good ghost advice.

"You told me before you were going to give the girl a talking-to because she was giving you such dirty looks," I said gently. "Maybe what she needs is kindness. The next time you see her, ask her what she wants. Offer to help her."

Lucy wrinkled her nose. "Ew, but she's a ghost."

"So? Some ghosts are here because they have something they still need to do, or answers they still need to find.

Wouldn't you feel good if you could help a ghost move on? Then she wouldn't bother anyone ever again."

Lucy's eyes brightened at this suggestion. "I'd be a hero to a ghost!"

"Exactly." I had to smile at how quickly Lucy was warming up to the idea of helping a ghost. I folded my arms on top of the table and said, "I happen to know two ghosts. Maybe you can talk to them for some advice."

Lucy nodded. "I remember Miss Clara said there are some ghosts where you work. I'd like that. Plus, you and Mister Damien still owe me a backstage tour. He promised."

Lucy had no idea Damien was her cousin, albeit twice removed or something like that. Still, she had instantly taken to him, and he seemed to feel the same toward her. In fact, I realized, it might be good for Damien to spend some time with Lucy. Like him, she was only beginning to discover her supernatural potential. Plus, she was just fun to be around.

I reached out with my little finger raised. "We'll do it next week."

Lucy curled her pinky around mine. "It's a deal."

Lucy and I chatted about ghosts, school, and the Halloween costume Mama was making for her while she sipped her hot chocolate. I helped myself to another cup of coffee, and by the time Lucy left, I was feeling pretty good. Like her, I didn't care for the "dead girl" I was helping, but I knew it was the right thing to do.

I kept that in mind as I drove to the fall festival shortly after lunch. The day was warm and sunny, and there wasn't a cloud in the sky. I had put on a long-sleeved floral blouse, and I regretted the decision halfway between the parking lot and the festival.

The festival was the most crowded I had seen it yet, and some of the narrower areas made me feel downright claustrophobic. Before I went to the Sanctuary booth, I headed for the maze to appease my curiosity.

Not surprisingly, the memorial to Annabelle had grown. It was about twice as big as the day before, and some of the flowers were clearly fresh. There was a line for the maze, and I even noticed someone taking a selfie with Annabelle's photo. I was still debating whether or not that was a tacky thing to do when Winston bustled past, a giant bag of hot dog buns in his arms.

"Oh, good, you're here to help. They're drowning at your booth!" Winston called as he passed.

I had no idea what he meant, so I hustled to the Sanctuary booth to find out. Daniel and Sam weren't having any kind of trouble, but there was a steady stream of people walking up to the table that was covered with flyers, discount coupons, and a werewolf-shaped candy bowl that would make growling noises whenever someone put their hand in it.

There were so many people around our booth that I couldn't find a clear path to walk up to the table. Instead, I skirted behind the row of booths and went through the back.

That's when I realized why the crowd was so big. There was a framed photo of Annabelle propped in the middle of the table, tilted so I could just see it from my vantage point. There was a vase of sunflowers next to it, as well as an oversized card that people were signing and writing messages on.

"Yes," I heard Daniel telling two women who were gazing at the photo with mournful expressions, "she worked for the Sanctuary, and we're so sad she's been taken from us."

Damien is going to flip when he hears about this.

"How's it going, gentlemen?" I called loudly.

Daniel turned and grinned at me. "Look at all these people!"

"We've almost sold out of the tickets we brought with us!" Sam added.

There was no way I would be able to grab Daniel for a little heart-to-heart chat about Annabelle when there were so many people at the booth. I had driven all the way to the festival for nothing.

Daniel turned his attention to a kid who was sinking his hand into the candy. When the bowl growled, the kid jumped and sent tart candies flying across the table. Daniel and Sam both laughed heartily, and Daniel produced a handful of chocolate candies for the kid. "Trick *and* treat!"

The kid and his family left, smiling, and I had to admit that the two temp workers had things well in hand.

Daniel stepped back and turned to me. "I know the thing for Annabelle is ridiculous," he said in a low voice, "but it's why we're so busy. Don't tell Damien, okay?"

That was something I couldn't promise, so I remained silent.

"I don't get it," Daniel continued. "All these people being so sad about her. They didn't even know her. And if they had known her, they wouldn't be sad that she's dead." Daniel laughed, enjoying his own joke.

"You're certainly not sad," I pointed out.

"I didn't like her," Daniel said simply. "I'm not going to fake being sad. What gets me is that she didn't even want to come back to Nightmare. It's almost like she knew what would happen."

"She probably didn't want to see Hal again," I speculated.

Daniel looked thoughtful. "It had to do with a guy, yeah. Some jealous girl accused Annabelle of stealing her boyfriend from her, and she even sent Annabelle really threatening notes."

My visit to the festival wasn't going to be for nothing, after all. "Kenzie!" I said.

Daniel gave me a strange look. "The gal that works here at the festival? She's not like that. No, Annabelle said she had bad blood with a bartender named, um, Hallie? Allie?"

"Callie?" I asked, horrified.

Daniel clapped his hands together. "Yes! That was it! Annabelle was being threatened by someone named Callie!"

CHAPTER NINETEEN

Sam called Daniel's name just then, and he returned his attention to the crowd. I simply stood there, my mouth agape and my eyes staring at the photo of Annabelle.

I had felt so good after my chat with Lucy. I was helping get justice for Annabelle's murder, and I would be able to pat myself on the back for doing the right thing. Except, at the moment, doing the right thing felt horrible.

Callie had claimed she wanted to tell me everything about her connection to Annabelle so I wouldn't put her on my suspect list. Had she told me a carefully crafted story, hoping I wouldn't find out about the threatening notes? And had her visit to the festival the night of Annabelle's murder been about more than proving some-thing to herself?

"Aw, man," I mumbled.

"I have a hard time believing it wasn't a murder." It was Kenzie, and she was standing at one side of the table.

I was about to answer that I was having a hard time believing it, too, then realized she wasn't talking to me but to Daniel. He laughed and said, "Same!"

Kenzie leaned over the table and handed Daniel a funnel cake that was half-buried in powdered sugar. "Here, I brought you a little treat."

"Thanks, sweetie. I'll repay the favor by taking you out for breakfast tomorrow."

"Sounds like a date."

Kenzie disappeared back into the crowd, and I couldn't help making a face of disgust while Daniel took a bite of his funnel cake. *Great, they're going to build a romantic relationship based on their mutual dislike of a fairy.*

I sighed, my thoughts going back to Callie. It wasn't looking good for her.

As I trudged to my car, I called Damien to fill him in. My call went right to voicemail, so I left a halting message explaining what Reyes had said about the colloidal silver, adding that whoever had killed Annabelle must have known she was a fairy. I didn't mention that the Nightmare Sanctuary booth was using her death as a way to sell more tickets. I figured Damien had enough to deal with as it was.

Instead of driving straight home, I just drove, with no idea where I was going. I didn't want to be indoors, and I didn't really want to be somewhere familiar. Getting lost seemed like the best way to escape from the world for a few hours. My car wasn't reliable, but if I broke down, I could call Lucy's dad, Nick, for a tow.

Getting lost was harder than I had expected. There were only so many roads around the outskirts of Nightmare, and when I hit the interstate, I went west to the next exit and tried another road. It just led me right past the festival again.

I should have gone hiking, I thought glumly. I had a terrible sense of direction when I was out in nature, and I would have done much better if I had tried to escape the world on foot.

Not knowing what else to do, I drove back to the motel, trudged up to my apartment, and flopped down onto my bed.

As it turned out, what I really needed was a nap,

because the next time I opened my eyes, the world outside was dimmer. I looked at my watch and yelped. "I gotta go!" I shouted to the room.

I changed into my Sanctuary T-shirt and a pair of black jeans in seconds, ran a brush through my hair while hoping I'd get to hide it under a pirate hat again, and dashed out the door.

I slid onto a bench in the dining room right as Justine was stepping up to the podium to start the family meeting. The hardest part of getting to work had been making my way from the staff parking area to the main entrance. There must have been one hundred people milling around outside the double doors, even though we didn't open for another hour.

As I had hoped, Justine assigned me to the lagoon vignette that night, saying that a temp could handle collecting tickets. That meant I didn't have to worry about the state of my hair or my face. My makeup hadn't survived my nap very well.

I ran to the costume room and changed into my pirate getup as soon as Justine dismissed us from the meeting. With that out of the way, I went in search of Clara. She wasn't in the dining room or the entryway, so I asked Justine, who was just coming from the hallway to Damien's office, where I might find her.

"In the cabin vignette, with Vivian," Justine said. "But before you go talk to Clara, you have to talk to Damien. He told me to send you in his direction."

Justine had a cardboard box full of fake severed limbs, and she shifted it so she could stand closer to me. "He's in a strange mood," she warned me. "He's not being a jerk, like usual, but he's tense. I felt like I was having a conversation with a bomb that might go off at any second."

"I'm not surprised," I said.

"Is this about his mom? I heard about the séance."

"His mom, and whatever supernatural power she might have passed down to him." I looked in the direction of the hallway and sighed. "At least, I hope that's all it is."

Justine wished me luck as I headed toward Damien's office, adding, "Maybe you can diffuse the bomb!"

I wasn't like Mama, who got vibes from people and could tell at a glance whether they were someone she wanted to be around. But, even with my total lack of ability in that department, I felt exactly what Justine had been talking about as soon as I crossed the threshold into the office.

Damien was sitting at his desk, focused on the screen of his laptop. He didn't look upset, and I noticed with some relief that he wasn't wearing his sunglasses. At the same time, though, there was an almost palpable tension in the room.

I stopped well before I reached the desk, feeling afraid. The energy in the room felt almost like a rubber band that had been stretched as far as it could go, and I worried that if I made one wrong move, it would snap. I wondered if it had to do with Damien's mom, or if my voicemail about the colloidal silver had thrown him into such a grim mood.

"Hi," I said cautiously.

Damien looked up at me and folded his hands on the desk. In a calm, even voice, he said, "I broke a vase, a wine glass, and a ceramic bowl."

This isn't about Annabelle, then. "Did you get upset thinking about your ex-fiancée?" I asked gently.

Damien was silent for a few moments. "No."

"Then what helped you channel your power?"

It could have been my imagination, but I could have sworn Damien's tanned skin turned just a shade darker. Was he blushing? "You don't have to tell me," I said quickly. "It's really none of my business. The important thing is that you're learning what emotions help you unleash your power."

"I also learned that I have to stop practicing at home. I'm tired of sweeping up shards." Damien smiled weakly, and I was surprised he was attempting humor. It seemed out of character for him.

Which means he wants to get as far away as he can from the discussion about his emotions.

"You're learning what it takes to move objects with your mind," I said, "which is great. The next step is learning to control that movement."

"The last thing I sent flying was the ceramic bowl. Even though I know it happened really quickly, I felt like I was watching it in slow motion. Before the bowl hit the wall, I thought how I wanted it to stop moving. It actually started to fall out of the air, but it was moving so quickly that it hit the wall, anyway."

"Still, that's progress! Well done, Damien!" I was over-doing it on the enthusiasm, and I was sure he could tell, but after the few days we'd all had, I figured he could use some positivity. *That's me, cheerleader to the supernaturals.*

"Thanks," Damien mumbled, seeming embarrassed again.

I could still feel that tension, and it seemed like everything I said was only adding to it. I took a careful step backward. "I appreciate the update," I said. "I'll catch up with you later."

"Wait," Damien said as I was turning to leave.

I kept my feet pointed in the direction of the door, but I twisted around so I could glance at him over my shoulder. "Yeah?"

Damien's voice was so low that I barely heard him. "Thanks for not giving up on me."

I just smiled in answer. There was no need for overblown enthusiasm this time around.

I felt the tension ease the second I was in the hallway, and I wondered if Damien's abilities were responsible for the weird feeling in his office. If he was subconsciously throwing objects across the room, maybe he was changing the energy of the space around him, too.

What had he been thinking about that made three objects go flying?

I was pondering what could possibly generate such a strong reaction, and why Damien wouldn't want to tell me about it, when I heard a shout. I recognized it as Zach's voice, and I saw him shoot out of the ticket office door. He was heading for the entryway.

"You can't just walk in!" Zach was shouting. A man was, in fact, walking right through the front door. The temp who had been assigned to ticket duty must have propped it open, and he was standing back, arms raised as if he were afraid the man might attack him.

I stopped where I was, because I had no desire to strut right into the middle of whatever was going on.

"He took a swing at me!" the temp shouted to Zach.

"Because you wouldn't let me in!" The man was glaring at the temp, his black hair sticking up in about fifty different directions and his hands balled into fists. His white T-shirt was half untucked, like he had been tugging on it.

"Sir," Zach said in a voice that told me he was exercising every bit of restraint he had, "you can't come in, because we aren't open yet, and you don't have a ticket."

"I can come in. I'm here to collect my girlfriend's things now that she's dead."

CHAPTER TWENTY

How many men did Annabelle have in her life? I wondered as I watched the wild-haired boyfriend. He had turned his ire on Zach, who was much more up to the challenge than the temp. The two of them looked like they might start throwing punches at any second, so I reluctantly forced myself to walk toward them.

"I'll take him to Damien," I said firmly. I stepped close to Zach and put my palm flat against his chest. For a brief moment, he continued to glare at Annabelle's boyfriend, and I heard a low growl in his throat. Zach was usually only a werewolf during the three days the moon was full, but if he got really angry or upset, he would temporarily turn.

Just like Damien's power is tied to heightened emotion.

I quickly filed that information away for later. The only thing that mattered at the present was how to prevent Zach from turning. I slid closer to him so my lips were nearly kissing his cheek. "Deep breaths," I said.

"Who does this guy think he—"

"In," I interrupted, "and out. Breathe with me. In, out." I had helped Zach calm himself once before, when he was so far into the turn that he was already beginning to physically change. That had been much scarier for me, and

I felt a flare of pride that I was handling the current situation so well.

Zach was wisely following my lead, taking measured breaths and forcing himself to relax. After a few long exhales, he peeled his eyes off the man and looked at me. His lips were set in a thin line, but he gave the tiniest of nods so I would know he was okay.

"I'm taking him to Damien," I said. "Take a quick break before you go back to the ticket window." I finally moved my hand from Zach's chest and gestured to Annabelle's boyfriend. "Follow me."

Once we were a few steps away, the man muttered, "Sorry about that. I'm a little on edge. My girlfriend just died, and I've had a long drive to get here."

"My condolences for your loss," I said. "What's your name?"

"Omar. Annabelle was my girlfriend."

"So you said. How long were you two together?"

"Since February. I've been driving since five a.m. to come get her stuff, and that stupid jerk—"

Omar's voice was growing louder and angrier, so I raised my voice to drown out his. "He didn't know who you were. I know you're grieving, but you don't have any reason to be angry, too. Zach was just doing his job."

"I guess."

Between cheering on Damien, breaking up a fight before it started, and lecturing Omar, I was starting to feel like less of a cheerleader and more of a mom. A mom dressed as a pirate, who knew how to talk a werewolf down from transforming.

My life really had gotten more interesting since arriving in Nightmare.

When I led the way into Damien's office, he looked up at me with surprise. "I thought you'd be getting settled into your spot in the lagoon—oh." He had caught sight of

Omar, who brushed past me and went right up to Damien's desk.

"I'm here to get Annabelle's things," he said. "That jerk at the front tried to keep me from coming in."

Damien's eyes flicked to mine. "This is Omar, Annabelle's boyfriend," I explained. "Zach didn't know who he was, so he understandably tried to keep Omar from coming inside."

The tension in the air was still there. Was this going to be the thing that snapped the rubber band?

"I'm sorry for your loss," Damien said. "I recently lost my father, so I can relate to your grief." Baxter was quite literally lost, not dead—at least, we all hoped not—but I figured Damien was doing what he could to calm Omar down. "Of course you'll want to take her things home. But first, why don't we sit down and talk."

Omar seemed to be as surprised as I was by Damien's politeness. As Omar settled into one of the oxblood leather chairs in front of the desk, I raised my eyebrows at Damien, but he either didn't notice my look or he was purposely ignoring me.

"Call me if you need my help," I said.

"I will." Damien was focused on Omar, but he spared me a brief glance. There was something almost mischievous in his expression.

He's going to try to get information out of Omar that might help us find Annabelle's killer, I thought. Damien was assisting me with the case.

There was no way I would have time to chat with Clara before we opened for the night, so I headed straight for the lagoon vignette. When I arrived, Malcolm and Mori were there, looking very out of place in the scene. They were huddled together with Theo at the foot of Seraphina's water tank.

"What's up?" I asked as I walked over.

"Did you hear?" Theo said. "Annabelle had a boyfriend, and he tried to fight his way in here. He and Zach nearly got into it!"

"Of course Olivia heard about it," Seraphina teased, flicking her fingers and sending a shower of drops down onto Theo's upturned face. "She's the one who broke up the fight!"

I raised my hands and laughed grimly. "No, they weren't fighting, but I think they were close to it. Zach was on the verge of turning."

Mori shuddered. "And you were right in the middle of it?"

"Zach calmed down pretty quickly."

Once my friends knew I was okay, they began to pepper me with questions about Omar. I answered as many as I could before the overhead lights went out, and we all had to get into place before guests started filing in.

Before Malcolm left through the door to the hidden paths that allowed staff to move around without being seen, he told me, "Don't worry. I'll keep an eye on him for you."

"Do you think he'll cause trouble?"

"He was dating the victim. I figure that makes him a suspect, so I assumed you'd want me to keep tabs on him."

I grinned at Malcolm. First Damien, and now Malcolm were jumping in to help with the case. I thanked him before he disappeared through the door, grateful that my friends were taking this as seriously as I was.

The next time I saw Malcolm was when he came to relieve me so I could have my break. As usual, Mori was in the dining room at the same time. I tried not to look at the cup in her hand, because I knew it had to be filled with blood. It was one aspect of being friends with vampires that I hadn't gotten used to yet, and I wasn't sure I ever would.

I was pleased when Clara joined us a few minutes later, and I could finally confide in her what Daniel had told me about Callie sending threatening notes to Annabelle. Not surprisingly, Clara was horrified at the idea of her sister being so vindictive. "I can't believe it," she said half a dozen times.

"I don't want to believe it, either, but I think I need to ask Callie about it." I took a deep breath and steeled myself for the next bit of news I had to share. "Officer Reyes called me this morning to tell me this wasn't a murder, because the lab report found no fatal substances in her system."

"But?" Clara asked, her violet eyes wide.

"But Annabelle did have a surprising amount of colloidal silver in her throat."

Clara blanched, and she brought her hands up to her face. "Oh! Oh, no. That poor girl. What a horrible way to go."

"I know silver repels fairies, so when Reyes told me that tidbit, I figured it must be how she died."

Clara nodded. "It would have been quick if it was enough silver, but I can't imagine how much it must have hurt. Poor, poor Annabelle. I didn't like her, but I would never wish for something so awful to happen to her."

"We need to talk to Callie," I said sadly.

"She's working tonight. Let's go get a drink while we're at it. I'm going to need a cocktail before I accuse my own sister of murder."

"We're just asking her about the threatening notes," I said, but Clara gave me a look that told me she had the same horrible fear that I did. Neither one of us wanted Callie to be a killer.

Mori, who had been sitting silently by us, suddenly elbowed me. "Watch out," she said under her breath.

Omar had just walked through the door, and he came

straight toward us. Mori quickly hid her cup behind her. Even though he had been dating a fairy, that didn't mean Omar knew Annabelle to be anything other than a human with surprisingly pointed ears and blue hair. Until we learned otherwise, we had to act like the supernatural world didn't exist, and that meant not having a cup of blood out in the open.

Omar gave me a solemn nod, then looked at Mori and Clara. "All three of you knew Annabelle?"

"Yes," we chorused.

"Thank you for being so kind to her in the short time she was here," Omar said. There wasn't a single hint of sarcasm in his tone. "Annabelle raved about what a cool job this was last year, and she was so excited to come back. She said she really felt at home at this haunted house."

I knew all three of us were self-conscious about the unearned praise. Mori stiffened, her full lips compressing into a tight line, and Clara twirled a lock of her silvery hair.

Clara was the one who spoke first, and after the news I had just relayed to her about the colloidal silver, I knew she was being sincere as she said, "We're so sorry about what happened. It's scary to think how easily, how quickly..." She stopped and took a deep breath. "Life is short, but Annabelle seemed like the type who lived it to the fullest."

"She definitely did." Omar ran a hand through his hair, which helped push some of the strands back into shape. He turned at the sound of Felipe's claws ticking across the stone floor, and it was that moment I realized it wasn't the first time I had seen him.

Omar was the guy who had come into the motel office to check in while I was working on my conjuring. At the time he had arrived, I had been focusing on getting answers about Annabelle's death.

Not only that, but when I had met Omar earlier that

evening, he had made it sound like he had just arrived in Nightmare. He had checked into Cowboy's Corral on Friday.

"Did you get to town yesterday?" I asked casually.

"I just got here," Omar said quickly.

No, you didn't, I thought. Why was Omar lying about when he had arrived? Had he gotten to town on Thursday, in time to kill his girlfriend, then laid low until his arrival at the motel on Friday?

Omar might be grieving, I realized, but he was also lying. The question was, why?

I absently bit into a potato chip and tried not to stare at Omar. I was dying to ask him more questions, but I couldn't think of one that would sound polite rather than accusatory.

Thankfully, Clara came to the rescue again. "Are you going to drive out to the fall festival? I hear there's a lovely memorial to Annabelle at the maze."

"I don't think I'm ready for that," Omar said. He ran his hand through his hair again. "Maybe tomorrow."

If he wasn't at the festival, then where has he been all day?

The dining room door banged open, and Malcolm swooped into the room, his black coat flying out behind him. As soon as he spotted me, he crooked a bony finger and said, "I need you. Now."

CHAPTER TWENTY-ONE

I immediately jumped up and hurried toward Malcolm. As I passed Omar, I heard him mutter, "Guy looks like the Grim Reaper."

"What's up?" I asked as I got closer to Malcolm.

"The crowd is so big that it's chaos out front. We need to set up stanchions for the ticket window, and I'm going to post the temp outside to direct people from the parking lot to the ticket line. I need you to stand at the door."

"But I'm a pirate," I said, gesturing at myself.

"Think of yourself as the pre-show."

When I got to the front entrance, I saw why Malcolm had used the word *chaos*. There were tons of people outside, but they were more of a crowd than any kind of cohesive line. I overheard someone ask the temp, who was tearing tickets, say, "Oh, this isn't the line for buying tickets?"

Malcolm and the temp set out to restore order, and it wasn't until I reached out to take the tickets for the next group in line that I realized I still had an unopened package of cookies in my hand. I quickly chucked them into the bin for ticket stubs. Zach would find himself a nice little snack when he sifted through the pile later.

Never in my life had I told so many people how to find the bathroom. I also did a lot of reassuring for people who looked scared at the mere idea of handing their ticket to a pirate.

Things were so busy I was barely looking at the people streaming through the door, and Hal was nearly past me before I recognized him. I opened my mouth to say something, but, after all, he had handed me a ticket. He had every right to be there, and judging by the laughter of the few people he was with, the guy was just trying to have a little fun. Maybe his friends had brought him to the Sanctuary as a distraction from his grief, though it seemed like a poor choice, since the very person Hal was grieving had been working there.

Great. How many of Annabelle's boyfriends are going to show up tonight?

Now and then, I spared a glance at the snaking line inside the entryway. Hal and his friends were talking together, and I even saw the hint of a smile on Hal's face at one point. By the time I spotted them approaching the door that marked the entrance of the haunt, my thoughts were less about Hal and more about the fact guests had to wait in three different long lines just to get scared. A line to buy tickets, a line to get in the door, and another line to get inside the actual haunt.

For someone like me, who maybe wasn't the most patient person in the world, that seemed more terrifying than anything inside the haunt itself.

When my watch read midnight on the dot, there was still a line of people coming through the door. Zach had closed the ticket window already, so I knew the line had to end at some point. It was almost twelve thirty before the last group entered the haunt. Outside, I could see a long line of brake lights as cars slowly made their way down the dirt road and back to the real world. Halloween was still more than a week away, so I could only imagine what was in store as we got closer to the holiday.

I leaned back against the door, closed my eyes, and yawned widely. I was already tired, and I wondered if Under the Undertaker's served coffee in addition to cocktails.

With another yawn, I straightened up and stretched. It was time to change back into my regular clothes and find Clara. Before I could do either of those things, though, I turned and saw Malcolm practically dragging Hal down the staircase. Hal was trying to squirm out of Malcolm's grip, but it was to no avail. Malcolm went right past me and through the door, Hal protesting loudly that he was being treated unfairly.

I, of course, followed. I couldn't help myself.

"You're lucky I'm letting you go," Malcolm was saying as I caught up. I had never heard him use such a severe tone before, and I was reminded of what Malcolm had told me about how dangerous he was.

"What's going on?" I asked. "Hal?"

"Who are you?" Hal was so surprised to hear me calling him by name that he stopped trying to escape Malcolm.

"I'm Olivia. Ella is a friend of mine, and I know your manager at The Lusty. Hal, what did you do?"

"I caught him upstairs," Malcolm growled. "He claims he was trying to find Annabelle's room."

"I just wanted to leave this in her memory," Hal said miserably. He raised a hand, and I saw a mangled rose in his grip. He must have had it tucked inside his hoodie while he had been waiting in line earlier. "I left flowers where she was killed, but this was where she lived. At least, for a few days." Hal turned his eyes toward the second story.

My ears had perked up at Hal's explanation. "You said where she was killed, but the police said she died of natural causes."

Hal snorted. "Do you really believe that? A woman like Annabelle, so beautiful and so perfect, always has jealous enemies."

I narrowed my eyes at Hal. "Like a woman whose boyfriend dumped her for Annabelle?"

"Yes, exact—no! I didn't mean… Don't bring Kenzie into this. She would never…"

Malcolm started to laugh, a quiet sound that was almost as ominous as the yelling he'd been doing just a few minutes before. When I looked at him, he just gave me a wry look. Instead of kicking Hal out, I was playing detective.

"Hal, come on, I'll walk you to your car," I said. Malcolm let go of him, but he trailed behind us as we headed toward the parking lot. "How did you get upstairs, anyway?"

"I slipped away from my friends and found a back staircase. This place was so busy that no one noticed me heading up there."

"If you had just asked for permission," I began, then stopped. Instead, I said, "You were working The Lusty's pop-up grill the night Annabelle died, right?"

"Yeah. I had gone over to talk to her earlier in the night, but she brushed me off. Just like she's been doing since last October."

That meant Annabelle had ditched the fling as soon as she had left Nightmare the previous Halloween, but clearly, Hal had been hanging onto the idea of it for an entire year.

I said generic soothing things as we approached Hal's car, about how he'd find somebody new and all the other useless advice people had told me in the wake of my divorce. Once he drove away, Malcolm stepped up to me.

"We should search the scene of the crime," he said.

"Why?" I asked with a shrug. "The police already went

over it, and after two days, surely any evidence there might have been is gone."

"Maybe the police missed something. Don't forget, they weren't looking for any signs of a supernatural crime."

"True. When should we go?"

"Tomorrow, early, before the festival is too crowded." Malcolm offered his arm to me. "Let's go in. I've got a poker rematch with Fiona that I need to get to."

Fiona was in the dining room, already shuffling a pack of cards, while she chatted with Clara and some others. As soon as Clara saw me, she said, "Let's go get this over with."

Mori, Theo, and Zach all rose with her.

"Are you all going with us?" I asked.

Theo clapped me on the shoulder. "We figured you two could use some moral support."

We said good night to Malcolm and Fiona and headed out, Felipe trotting along next to us. I insisted on dashing to Damien's office to ask if he wanted to go with us, which made everyone groan. "He'll say no, anyway," I assured them.

I was right. Damien didn't have the slightest interest in going out with us, but I was relieved that the tense feeling in his office had subsided. I didn't know if that metaphorical rubber band had snapped sometime during the night, or if he had simply calmed down enough that the energy of the space had shifted back to almost normal. Either way, I felt confident I could leave him alone and not worry that all the books on the shelves were suddenly going to take flight.

We chose to walk to the bar, partly because it was such a cool, pleasant night, but also because Felipe was clearly ready to stretch his legs. He ran circles around us as we walked, sometimes darting off into the underbrush. Once, he came back smacking his chops, though I couldn't imagine what he had eaten.

Usually, heading to Under the Undertaker's was fun, but given our reason for going, we were pretty subdued as we trooped down the spiral staircase into the basement-level bar.

Clara insisted that we get our drinks before I asked Callie any questions. "For one thing, I need a drink before the drama," she said. "For another, I don't want my sister spitting in our cocktails because we accused her of murder."

Both of Clara's arguments seemed perfectly logical, even though I reminded her, again, that we weren't accusing anyone of murder.

In short order, we all had drinks in front of us. Mori and Theo were both having blood, and I avoided looking at their glasses as much as possible.

Clara took a long sip of her drink, which was something fruity with a pineapple slice in it. "Okay," she said, waving toward Callie, who was delivering drinks to another table, "now that I've got my drink, you can ask her anything you like."

The next time Callie passed near our table, I called her over. Mori, Theo, and Zach all immediately rose and wandered toward the bar against one wall, so Callie wouldn't feel like she was being questioned in front of an audience.

"Do you have a minute to sit with us?" I asked.

Callie's expression turned wary. "This is something about Annabelle, isn't it?"

"I'm afraid so."

Callie sat down, her hands clamped together. "Okay, then."

"Callie, we know you were sending threatening notes to Annabelle," I said.

"What?" Callie looked genuinely confused. "What are you talking about? I never did anything like that."

"Why would Annabelle have said that if it weren't true?" I wondered aloud. I stared down into my drink, like the answer might be in there.

"She probably didn't say it," Callie said angrily. She pointed to somewhere over my shoulder. "I'm willing to bet money that jerk made it up."

I turned and saw Daniel sitting a short distance away.

CHAPTER TWENTY-TWO

"Daniel is the one who told me," I confirmed. "I had no idea you two knew each other."

"Oh, yeah," Callie said, glaring in his direction. "He hung out here a lot when he was in town last Halloween. He hit on me at least half a dozen times every night."

"Ew, he's so not your type," Clara said, wrinkling her nose.

"Also," I added, "couldn't the guy take a hint?"

"Trust me, the second he walked in here this season, I shut him down immediately," Callie said. "He didn't get one word out of his mouth before I told him that if he hit on me even once, I would have him thrown out."

"Good for you!" Clara turned toward the bar and called to Mori, then gestured the three of them back over. Once they were seated, she asked Callie, "Do you think Daniel made that up about you threatening Annabelle because you rejected him?"

"Probably," Callie said. "I can't imagine why else he would lie about me like that."

"Only one way to find out," I said. I got up and marched right over to the table where Daniel and two other temps were sitting. "May I please speak to you privately?" I asked him.

Daniel looked at me, then toward our table, then back at me. "I didn't say a word to her," he said defensively.

"I know, but I still need to speak to you."

Daniel looked toward his friends and rolled his eyes dramatically, then looked at me and sighed heavily. "Fine." He made a show of putting down his drink and standing up slowly. "I was trying to relax after a hard night of work, you know."

"Me, too," I quipped. I led Daniel to a dark corner that was partially screened by a long length of midnight-blue silk hanging from the ceiling. If I was going to lecture the guy, I would at least give him some privacy.

Before I could start my lecture, though, Daniel raised a hand. "Look, I'm just here to have a drink with my co-workers. I swear, all I did was give her my drink order."

"That's not what I want to talk to you about," I said. "When you told me Annabelle was getting threatening notes from someone named Callie, you failed to mention that you know her. You even pretended not to remember her name."

One of Daniel's shoulders twitched in a halfhearted shrug. "I really couldn't remember her name. I always think of her as the hot fairy. Besides, I didn't think it mattered that I know her."

"Of course it matters. You told me Callie was threatening Annabelle, but Callie says she did no such thing. Did you make that story up because Callie wouldn't go out with you?"

Daniel's demeanor changed in an instant, his flippant attitude suddenly turning defensive. "I didn't make it up! Annabelle really was getting threats. She even showed me one of the notes. It said something about always watching her and making sure she couldn't hurt anyone else."

"And, what, Callie signed her name to it?"

"Obviously she wouldn't do that. The note wasn't signed." Daniel hesitated, then sighed again, but this time, it was in defeat rather than defiance. "I don't actually know who was sending the notes to Annabelle, and neither did she. She had told me about her and Callie having a history, and that Callie hated her, so I just assumed she was the one behind it."

I crossed my arms. "Callie was far from the only person who didn't like Annabelle, as you well know. If I had passed along your info to the police…"

"They wouldn't have cared," Daniel finished for me. "They said Annabelle died because she had a heart problem."

Was Daniel really that naive? "She died because she was a fairy, and someone fed her silver."

Daniel's face went slack. He looked over his shoulder, toward the occupied tables, then back at me. "Are you serious?"

I nodded, not sure whether I believed he was really shocked by the news or just playing a part. Daniel had falsely identified Callie as the one threatening Annabelle, and while he might have simply made a mistaken assumption, like he claimed, he also might have done it for revenge on Callie.

There was a third possibility, too. Maybe Daniel had killed Annabelle, and he wanted fingers to point at anyone but himself.

Daniel swore under his breath. "Since the police don't think it was murder, I'm guessing they don't know about the notes. You should look through Annabelle's stuff and find them. Maybe you can match the handwriting, or find something in the text that will help you figure out who really did write them."

That was a solid idea, but Omar had already arrived to pack up his girlfriend's things, which meant he had the notes. Instead of telling Daniel that, I just waved my hand toward his table. "Thanks for coming clean," I said.

"I just assumed Callie had to be the one behind the threats," Daniel said. "I don't want her to think I was trying to make her look bad. She might kick me out."

"Then you should tell her you were mistaken and apologize," I suggested. "Maybe she'll think a little less badly of you."

I wasn't going to miss Daniel when he went home after the Halloween season.

I returned to my friends, who looked at me expectantly. "Annabelle really was getting threatening notes, and based on some things she had said to Daniel, he mistakenly assumed Callie had written them," I said.

"Then who did write them, and why?" Mori took a long sip of her blood as she looked toward Daniel thoughtfully.

"Let's hope we can find out," Clara said. "I don't want Callie dragged into this, so the faster we clear her name, the better. It's only a matter of time before word spreads through the supernatural community that this was a murder."

"How would anyone outside the Sanctuary find out about the silver?" I asked.

Theo laughed grimly. "Word has a way of traveling. And, if the supernatural community where Annabelle is from has any doubt about her death being natural, they'll get the same details from the police that you did, Olivia. All it takes is one vampire to mesmerize an officer, and they'll spill every detail."

"I guess we have more work to do, then." I raised my glass. "But first, it's been a really long day, and I'd like to think about something other than Annabelle for the next hour or so."

Zach raised his mug of beer and clinked it against my

glass. "Then have I got a story for you! Rumor has it that Damien showed up at the Sanctuary the other day with a woman!"

"What?" Mori asked, her eyes wide. "He actually found someone who wants to date him?"

"No way!" Theo said.

I wasn't sure what I wanted to do most: glower at Zach or take a long drink. I opted for the latter, but halfway through my sip, Zach added, "She's pretty sexy, too."

I started to laugh, which turned into a cough as I choked on my drink. Once I swallowed, I hissed, "Zach!"

"What's wrong, Olivia?" he asked. "Can't take a compliment?"

Clara, Mori, and Theo all turned to me. Mori had a little smile on her face, the tips of her fangs just showing.

"Damien gave me a ride to work," I clarified.

"Boring!" Theo shouted. "I demand you make up something more interesting!"

"More scandalous!" Mori added.

Clara just laughed, and even though I eventually shifted the subject to something else, every now and then, one of them would give me a sly look.

On the plus side, at least I didn't think about Annabelle or murder for a long time.

I woke up on Sunday morning feeling like I needed a few more hours of sleep, but I was also anxious to get to— as Malcolm had called it—the scene of the crime. I had agreed to pick him up shortly before ten, but since I was moving a little slower than usual, it was a few minutes after ten when I finally parked at the Sanctuary.

I was surprised to find both Malcolm and Clara waiting for me. Clara was yawning as I walked up. "We didn't drink much last night, but we sure stayed out late," she remarked.

"We needed to let off some steam," I said, trying to stifle my own yawn.

Malcolm, at least, looked the same as ever. He wished me a good morning, then added, "I think we should stop and get coffee on the way to the festival. You two are going to make me start yawning, and I'm not even tired."

"Good idea," I said. "Coffee, then crime scene."

"I hope we find something," Clara said. "Otherwise, I lost sleep for nothing."

"Are you joining us?" I asked, surprised.

Clara squared her shoulders. "I have to do what I can for Callie. And, since I'm a fairy, I might spot something where Annabelle died that you wouldn't. Something that might seem completely ordinary to you would stand out to me, if it was fairy related."

"Like more silver sitting around," I speculated.

It wasn't until we were in the car that I suddenly said, "Oh!" My hand strayed up to the necklace Damien had given me. The delicate charms on it—a cross and a penta-gram—had powerful protection spells on them, and Baxter had given it to Lucille to keep her safe. When it became clear that I had a knack for getting into trouble, Damien had given the necklace to me. "Clara, does my necklace bother you since it's silver?"

I looked in the rearview mirror so I could see Clara, who was sitting in the back seat. She scrunched up her face. "It doesn't really bother me, because it's not a lot of silver. People wearing silver jewelry come through the Sanctuary all the time, but as long as I don't touch it, I'm okay. I'm normally a hugger, but I have to be careful with you, Olivia."

I chewed on my lip as I considered that information. "Do you want me to stop wearing it?"

"Absolutely not," Malcolm said. He looked at me like I

had a death wish. "That necklace is powerful, and you need all the help you can get to stay safe."

Clara giggled. "What Malcolm said. Besides, didn't you get it from your *boyfriend*?" She said the last word in a singsong tone, and I just groaned in answer.

As Malcolm had predicted, there weren't a lot of cars in the field at the fall festival that early on a Sunday morning. Clara and I had coffees in hand as the three of us climbed out of the car and started our walk toward the maze.

"Should we let Winston know we're here?" I asked.

"I don't think we should," Malcolm said slowly. "If he's at all involved in Annabelle's death, he won't like the idea of us going into the maze to look for clues. Today, we're just three people out to have a good time at the Nightmare Fall Festival. Three totally normal, boring people who think ghosts and monsters are just made up."

"Fairies aren't monsters," Clara said pointedly.

"Ghosts, monsters, and sweet supernatural creatures," Malcolm corrected himself.

"Much better."

When we reached the entrance to the maze, Malcolm pulled cash out of his pocket and paid the entry fee for all three of us. I felt a chill as soon as we entered the maze. There wasn't a cloud in the sky, but even in broad daylight, I didn't like the place. The corn was so much taller than me that I felt trapped between the rows.

"I don't know if I can find my way back to where Annabelle died," I said when we came to the first path that veered off to one side.

Malcolm stopped, lifted his face to the sky, and sniffed. He then turned slightly and sniffed again. "This way."

Clara and I gave each other confused glances as we followed Malcolm. He seemed to sense our curiosity, because he called over his shoulder, "The smell is mostly gone, but there's a hint of it left."

"The smell of what?" I asked.

"Death."

Malcolm stopped and smelled the air each time we had to decide which path to follow, and after five or six turns, he said, "We're here."

Clara and I bent at the waist and began to look at the dirt. There were sneaker prints, bits of cornstalks that had fallen to the ground and been trampled, and some dead weeds poking out of the hard earth.

There was also something red and yellow, nearly obscured by loose dirt. I crouched down and picked it up. "Just a candy wrapper," I said, disappointed. "Some kid must have dropped it."

Clara leaned over my shoulder. "Honey candy! Fairies love honey." She reached out and plucked the wrapper from my fingers, then immediately dropped it with a hiss. "There's silver on it! The candy must have been laced with it!"

CHAPTER TWENTY-THREE

Clara sucked in her breath and blew on her fingertips, which were bright red. Malcolm produced a crisp white handkerchief and handed it to her wordlessly. As Clara wiped her fingers clean, she said in a shaky voice, "We found the murder weapon."

"The killer must have mixed the colloidal silver into the candy," I said.

"And they must have known Annabelle would eat the candy without hesitation. Honey and candy, all in one package? Irresistible." Clara was staring at the wrapper with disdain.

"Which only confirms my guess that whoever killed her knew she was a fairy." I shook my head sadly. "Of all our suspects, only Callie and Daniel know about our world. Or, possibly, Omar."

"My sister didn't kill anyone," Clara said through clenched teeth.

"I don't think she did, either." I stared down at the candy wrapper. "If the paper hurt you, then wouldn't it have hurt Annabelle, too? There's no way she could have unwrapped it and touched the candy without knowing it was laced with silver."

"Annabelle liked putting on a show, remember?" Malcolm pointed out. "She probably opened her mouth and let her killer feed it to her. In fact, I'll bet her killer was counting on that. She was never meant to touch the wrapper."

I thought of Annabelle's flirtatious giggling just moments before her death. In my imagination, I could practically see her tilting her chin up and opening her mouth to be fed candy. "Could the candy have hidden enough silver to be deadly?" I asked Clara.

"Probably not. The silver in the candy would have been incredibly painful, and it would have weakened her instantly. Of course, she would have known something was wrong as soon as it was in her mouth, but her killer probably covered her mouth and nose until she swallowed it."

I shuddered at the mental image. In addition to the silver, Annabelle had also been half-suffocated, if Clara's speculation was right.

"After that, it would have been easy for whoever did this to make her drink more colloidal silver. She wouldn't have been able to fight back." Clara shook her head sadly.

Officer Reyes had even described it as a dropperful. Her killer had probably shot it right down her throat, and there was nothing Annabelle could do to prevent it.

I looked at Clara and Malcolm. "What do we do now? Do we take this wrapper to Reyes and ask the police to fingerprint it? He'll laugh us out of the station for suggesting Annabelle was killed by the colloidal silver."

"We could buy the same kind of candy and offer it to suspects to see if one of them hesitates or acts guilty," Malcolm suggested.

"Maybe we don't need to buy it," I said. "We just need to know where the killer bought it. There can't be that many places around town that are selling it. Maybe someone at the supermarket or one of the convenience stores would remember who they sold it to."

Of course, I realized, that only worked if the candy

had been purchased in Nightmare. Daniel could have bought it before arriving in town. Omar could have done the same. He was obviously up to something, since he was pretending to have arrived in Nightmare on Saturday, even though I had seen him at Cowboy's Corral on Friday.

My coffee cup was empty by then, so I used the edge of my shoe to push the candy wrapper into the cup, then secured the plastic lid. That way, we had the evidence with us, but it wouldn't be able to hurt Clara again.

Since the maze was supposed to be one way, we had to continue on until we found the exit. I hated every second of it, but the few people we saw seemed to be enjoying the challenge. I was willing to swear that the air was easier to breathe as soon as we walked out of the maze.

The three of us strolled past the booths, partly because Clara was on the prowl for a funnel cake and partly because I wanted to see what kind of candy was being offered at the various booths and games that were set up. Not surprisingly, plenty of them had honey candy in their bowls, alongside the other usual treats. Nightmare was a small town, but finding all the stores selling the candy might be harder than I had thought.

Clara was making the same observations I was, because we were cruising past the dunk tank as she said quietly, "The killer could have gotten the candy here, too."

"And then what?" I stopped and considered that theory. "They showed up with a bottle of colloidal silver, but they didn't get the candy to put it in until they arrived here? You said fairies love honey, so the choice of candy was no accident. This was premeditated."

"Watch out," Malcolm said under his breath.

I looked up to see Winston and Kenzie walking in our direction. "Hi!" I said brightly. Too brightly. I sounded so fake.

Kenzie was instantly on her guard. "Are you three working the Sanctuary booth today?"

"No," Clara said. I noticed that her tone was bright and happy without sounding fake. I would have to ask her how she did it, but I suspected it might be some kind of fairy ability. "Actually, we wanted to come out and have some fun. Halloween is Malcolm's favorite holiday, and he loves fall festivals."

"It's true." Malcolm lifted his top hat, giving just a brief glimpse of his bald head, and smiled at Kenzie. "It's nice to see you again, Kenzie."

"Nice to see you, too."

Judging by the way Kenzie was staring at Malcolm, it was not nice for her, at all. To be fair, though, Malcolm did look a bit intimidating thanks to his height and his pale, gaunt features.

Winston chuckled. "Malcolm doesn't love Halloween. He *is* Halloween. Look at him, head-to-toe spooky!"

Malcolm straightened his hat on his head and smiled proudly. "Thank you. We had a delightful time in the maze just now."

Kenzie's eyes grew even wider, and she took a step back. Then, she pitched backward, her arms flailing. Winston reached out and grabbed her around the waist, and Malcolm's hand shot forward to grasp Kenzie's. Between the two men, they were able to keep Kenzie from landing flat on her back.

"What the...?" Kenzie shook off both Malcolm and Winston and turned around, looking at her feet. She pointed at a small jack-o'-lantern that was half smashed on the ground. "That wasn't there when we walked up. I stepped right on it, and that's why I almost fell over."

No one had been close enough to put a jack-o'-lantern at Kenzie's feet. Even if they had been, the three of us who were facing her would have noticed.

"Maybe it fell off the pile and rolled over here," Winston said, pointing at a nearby arrangement of hay bales and pumpkins. "Or, someone walking past accidentally kicked it in our direction."

Kenzie was staring at Malcolm again, like he was somehow responsible. "Enjoy the festival," she muttered before stomping off.

"Sorry about that," Winston said. "She's had a long week. We all have."

We all made polite responses, but as soon as Winston had walked away, too, I looked at Clara and Malcolm. "Where did that little pumpkin come from?"

"No idea, but Kenzie was right. It wasn't there when they walked up." Malcolm was frowning down at the half-grin that remained intact on the pumpkin.

Clara made a high-pitched noise. "This place is giving me the creeps. Let's go."

When we got back to my car, Clara insisted that I stash the coffee cup containing the candy wrapper in my trunk, so there was absolutely no way she could come into contact with it.

We discussed what we had learned about how the silver was delivered, but we didn't get any further in figuring out who had done it in the first place, or why. Daniel was still at the top of my suspect list, since he had known Annabelle was a fairy and blamed her for getting kicked out of his old apartment. Unfortunately, Callie's name was just under Daniel's.

"Can we have Tanner and McCrory do some snooping in Daniel's room?" I said as I turned right at the old gallows. "They've done some spying for us before."

"Do you really think he's the one who did it?" Clara's voice trembled. "What if he goes after Callie, too?"

"Tell her not to take candy from anyone, especially him," I advised.

"I think getting the ghosts involved is a good idea," Malcolm said, "but you would need to run it past Damien first. Since he's the de facto owner of the Sanctuary, that makes Daniel his responsibility. We don't exactly have a human resources department here, but we do have ethics."

"Right," I agreed grudgingly. "Tanner and McCrory might be able to take a peek at Daniel's room, but only when he's not in it, because even suspects deserve a little privacy. And since the ghosts can't physically move objects, they might not turn up much."

I had pulled up in front of the Sanctuary by then, so I put the car in park and turned so I could see both Clara and Malcolm. "Thanks for helping today. We learned some really valuable information."

"I'll ask Damien about Tanner and McCrory, though I don't think they'll be able to do a lot for us," Clara said. "I need to talk to him about some prop repairs, anyway."

"Thanks. See you two tonight."

Clara climbed out of the car, but Malcolm didn't budge. His expression looked strained, and he cleared his throat three times, all while avoiding looking at me.

"Is there something you want to tell me?" I asked.

"I don't want to, but I need to." Malcolm finally met my eyes. "No matter how afraid I might be of telling you what I am, it's time."

I suddenly felt afraid, too. For months, I had been so curious to know what kind of supernatural creature Malcolm was. But after he had said he used to be the most dangerous thing in the Arizona Territory, I wasn't sure I wanted to know anymore. At the same time, though, I knew it was better to hear the truth.

"Go ahead," I said, steeling myself.

Malcolm shook his head. "Not here. Let's go to Cowboy's Corral. Mama needs to hear it, too. She *deserves* to hear it, and I only want to tell my tale once."

CHAPTER TWENTY-FOUR

I looked at Malcolm almost as much as I looked at the road while I drove us to Cowboy's Corral. It was a good thing I had driven the route so many times, or I probably would have veered off into a mesquite tree or a cactus.

Instead of parking at the back corner of the motel, by my apartment, I pulled up in front of the office. Malcolm climbed out of the passenger seat grimly, and I took a deep breath before getting out and following him through the glass door.

Mama was sitting at the desk behind the check-in counter, only the top of her hair visible, but as soon as the bell over the door tinkled, she rose with a warm smile on her face.

The smile faded as soon as she saw Malcolm. "You have bad news," she said.

"Not exactly," Malcolm answered. He laughed sadly. "You are a perceptive one, Mama. I didn't come here to give you news, though. Rather, I came to tell you a story. My story."

The color drained out of Mama's face. *She knows, too,* I thought. *We both know Malcolm is dangerous, even though neither of us knows what he is.*

Mama came out from behind the counter and walked right past us. She locked the door, flipped the sign hanging in the window from *Come On In!* to *Be Right Back!*, and sat down in one of the chairs. With a wave of her arm, she directed Malcolm and I to sit, too. I settled into the chair next to Mama, but Malcolm pulled his chair around so he was facing the two of us. He sat down, twisted his hands together in his lap, then stood again.

Malcolm began to pace, slowly, between the counter and the front door. "I said a couple days ago that I was once the most dangerous thing around, and it's time for both of you to know exactly what I am."

"Malcolm, dear," Mama interrupted, "we've known each other for a long time. Whatever you're about to say won't change how I feel about you."

"We'll see." Malcolm was at the door, and he reached up to touch the bell delicately. "I'm originally from New York City. But, as word spread that there were fortunes to be made in the West, I moved to Colorado. The mine I was working stopped giving gold only six months after I had arrived. I had heard there was a new mine opening in the Arizona Territory, so I decided to head there."

Malcolm paused in his pacing and looked at us. "I left Colorado with three other miners. It was March, and we were optimistic that we could get over the mountains without too much trouble. Unfortunately, there was a late-season blizzard. We were snowed in, with no town and no help for miles."

I tentatively raised my hand, like a kid in school. "Did you already know you were supernatural at that point?"

"I was completely human then. I wasn't born supernatural." Malcolm sighed. "And as humans, my companions and I were in real danger of freezing or starving to death out there in the wild. Simon went first, because he had never really recovered from a bout of rubella, and he was weaker than the rest of us. Then Harry broke his leg while foraging for food. We found him and brought him back to our camp, but there wasn't much we could do for him.

"Then the food ran out. I could feel myself getting more and more desperate, and by the fifth day, Harry was on the verge of succumbing to his injury. I grabbed my gun, and I told myself I was helping him, ending his misery, but the truth was, I was simply hungry."

I pressed my hands to my face, horrified. Malcolm's mouth twitched, and he dropped his head. "I'm not proud of what I did, but Harry's death allowed me to live."

"And the fourth companion?" Mama asked, her voice strained. "What happened to him?"

"He ran out into the snow one night and never came back. He said he'd rather freeze than be anywhere close to someone who was cursed. I thought he was being overly dramatic, but in the weeks following the blizzard, I began to change. I got painful cravings for—" Malcolm blew out his breath and resumed his pacing. "It's a Native American legend, but like most legends, there's a basis in fact. I had eaten another human, and I was transforming into a monster because of it. By the time I made it to that mining camp in the Arizona Territory, I wasn't there to pan for gold. I was there to feed."

"On people," I said flatly.

Malcolm nodded. "It wasn't until years later, when I met Baxter, that I would learn there was a name for what I was. Wendigo. Baxter saved my life. He taught me to act like a human again."

"If you're a wendigo," Mama said, "then Baxter saved a lot more lives than yours by teaching you to control your cravings."

My eyes had been glued to Malcolm's face, but Mama's comment made me turn to her. "You've heard of this kind of creature?"

"I thought they were just a legend, like Malcolm said. But yes, I've heard of them, and they're ruthless."

"But we can be tamed, with enough time and discipline," Malcolm said. "It took Baxter the better part of fifty years to get me under control."

"Fifty years?" I repeated. "When did you two meet?"

"Oh, sometime around eighteen seventy-nine."

"You're both so old." I leaned forward, my horror forgotten for the moment. "And you're both day-walkers who look mostly human. But you say you and Baxter aren't the same kind of creature?"

Malcolm was shaking his head vehemently before I had finished talking. "No, Baxter isn't a wendigo. I don't know what he is, but he's not like me. I've never seen him use any kind of supernatural power, though I suspect his ability to keep all of us together, peacefully, is a manifestation of it. He has a will that is beyond anything I've seen in a normal human."

Mama shut her eyes. "Bless your heart, Malcolm. No wonder you didn't want us to know."

"Whatever you've done in the past, your supernatural power helped us today," I said.

"I was coming to that. One of the perks of being a wendigo is that I can smell humans from a long way off. It's like my senses heightened to turn me into a predator. My hearing, my vision, my strength, all of it is honed to track down a human. And, for me, there's a distinct difference between the smell of a living human and a dead one."

"You're talking about the death stench you used to find the spot where Annabelle was murdered," I said.

"Precisely. And tracking down the spot where Annabelle died made me realize there are things the two of you should know about Baxter and Lucille, which is why I decided to tell you the truth about me. When Lucille

162

went missing, I searched for her scent all over Nightmare. I couldn't detect her, either living or dead. Now, of course, we know Lucille likely transformed into a non-corporeal entity by choice."

"And Baxter?" Mama prompted.

"I never caught a hint of his death stench, but his living scent? It led me down a dirt road out beyond the Sanctuary, then abruptly ended. It was like something had swooped down out of the sky and taken him."

"Or he was thrown into a vehicle." I stood and began to pace right next to Malcolm. "He might have been kidnapped."

"That's one of our theories, though I didn't see any tire tracks when I was on the road. Whoever took him might have covered their tracks really well."

"Or they did swoop down out of the sky, like you said," Mama suggested. "A number of supernatural creatures can fly or levitate."

"Or fly a helicopter," I pointed out. "But why would they take Baxter?"

Malcolm spread his hands. "We don't know, because we don't know what Baxter is. All I do know is that Baxter is alive, or was, when he went missing. I also know that Lucille was right: you and Damien are going to be the ones to find him."

"Why us?" Lucille's message still made no sense to me.

"Why not?" Malcolm countered. "Your conjuror skills and Damien's powers are going to work together in a way that none of us can anticipate."

"Except my sister did anticipate it," Mama said, both pride and sadness in her voice. "She knew before Olivia ever arrived in Nightmare that she and Damien are going to do extraordinary things together."

Oh, wow, no pressure.

"Speaking of Damien," I said, anxious to change the subject, "Mama, didn't you two have lunch today?"

"He took me to Barton's Barn for brunch. It was lovely, though that man is tightly wound. Goodness, he needs to learn to relax."

"Agreed."

Mama got up, walked over to Malcolm, and pulled him into a hug. "Like I said, this doesn't change the good friend you've always been to me and Lucille." Mama let Malcolm go and grabbed a plastic jack-o'-lantern candy bucket off the countertop. "Here, help yourselves. A little something sweet will make us all feel better after that heavy conversation."

Malcolm and I both looked inside the bowl and groaned.

There was a piece of honey candy sitting right on top of the pile.

CHAPTER TWENTY-FIVE

On the drive back to the Sanctuary, Malcolm sat stiffly in the passenger seat, his head turned toward the window.

"You're my friend," I told him. "Knowing your story hasn't changed that."

Malcolm let out a long sigh, and he seemed to shrink by a couple of inches. "Thank you."

Damien's car was at the Sanctuary, so instead of dropping Malcolm off, I parked and walked inside with him. Before we parted in the entryway, I gave Malcolm a hug, just to reassure him. His past was horrifying, but that didn't change the fact he had been one of my first friends in Nightmare, and he had always made me feel welcome there.

The door to Damien's office was closed, so I knocked. Instead of him telling me to come in, I heard footsteps, then Damien opened the door. "Oh, Olivia. Not who I was expecting."

Damien returned to his seat at the desk, and I settled into one of the leather chairs. For a moment, I was too consumed by my own thoughts to say anything. Between the candy wrapper and Malcolm's story, my brain was moving at full speed.

"You wanted to see me?" Damien prompted. He didn't say it impatiently. Instead, he seemed curious.

"Do you know what Malcolm is?" I asked.

"Yeah, I've known since I was a teenager, after my power first manifested. My father had me sit down for a lecture from Malcolm about how dangerous it is to be supernatural."

"That doesn't seem fair. Malcolm is so different from a lot of supernatural creatures. Your dad shouldn't have compared your situation to Malcolm's." In fact, I realized, other than his heightened senses, Malcolm didn't seem to have anything I would call "powers." The poor guy was supernatural, and all he really had to show for it was a long life and a craving for people.

"My father wanted me to feel like I was a monster, so I wouldn't be tempted to explore my abilities."

"How ironic that we're going to need those abilities to find the man who taught you to bury them." Before I could dive into a commentary on Baxter's parenting style, I heard several pairs of footsteps in the hallway. I leaned to the side so I could peek behind me, and I was surprised to see Zach showing Winston and Kenzie into the office.

"We meet again," Winston said to me. "Did you enjoy the festival this morning?"

"I survived the maze," I said. Immediately, I realized it sounded like I was cracking a joke about Annabelle's death, so I quickly added, "Mazes give me claustrophobia, but Malcolm did a good job of guiding us through."

"He's not here yet," Kenzie said, looking around.

"You're a few minutes early." Damien grabbed a stack of papers on his desk and shoved them into a drawer. To me, he said, "Omar has asked for a meeting with the three of us. He wants to get as many details about Annabelle's death as he can. It's possible he thinks there's more to it than natural causes."

He's not wrong. Damien and I know it, but do Kenzie and Winston?

"In that case," I said, rising, "I'll leave you all to it. Winston, Kenzie, nice seeing you both again." It really wasn't, but I figured it didn't hurt to be polite.

I reached the doorway at the same time as Omar, who was just coming in. I stepped back and turned sideways to make room for him, and as he entered, I saw a framed photo on the built-in bookcase slide a few inches. I quickly looked at Damien, but he was greeting Omar and didn't notice my glance.

Damien's eyes weren't glowing, and he didn't give any outward appearance of being upset. But, if he had subconsciously made the photo move by itself, then there was some kind of turmoil going on under the surface. I needed to keep an eye on him. It was one thing for him to psychically fling objects across the room when I was around, but it would be a whole different issue if he did it in front of people who didn't know about the supernatural world.

Besides, somebody might get hurt.

"I was there that night, too," I spoke up. "Maybe I should stay, so I can help put the pieces together."

Damien's mouth twitched upward, and he brought a hand up to cover his smile. He thought I was staying so I could investigate the murder, and he was laughing at me. All the better, I realized. If he thought I was there to catch a killer, then he wouldn't suspect I was really there to keep him calm. Omar and I stood while Winston and Kenzie sat in the chairs. I made sure my vantage point gave me a good look at Damien's face.

Omar began to ask questions, directing them mostly to Winston. He wanted to know why Annabelle had been assigned to the maze, how she had been acting before work that night, and whether or not anyone had looked suspicious. I chimed in here and there, but it was the same information we had been going over again and again.

There had been nothing in the hours leading up to Annabelle's death that had rung any alarm bells.

Even when I was talking, I was keeping a close eye on Damien. His eyes still weren't glowing, though he was listening intently to the conversation. At one point, he glanced in my direction, and I mouthed, "You okay?" Unfortunately, Damien had already looked away.

Omar also asked a lot of questions about Annabelle's life at the Sanctuary, but since she had only been there for a couple of days that season, there wasn't much we could say. I briefly toyed with the idea of bringing up the scene between Winston and Annabelle at the front entrance, but that would only make Winston look guilty, and it would probably throw the Sanctuary's involvement in the Nightmare Fall Festival into jeopardy yet again.

As the conversation began to wind down, though, there was one subject no one had mentioned yet. "Omar," I began, "when you packed up Annabelle's belongings, did you happen to find any threatening notes? Apparently, someone was bitter about her stealing away their boyfriend."

"Don't look at me," Kenzie said immediately. Of course, that just made us all look at her, and she stared around at us defiantly.

"I'm not accusing you of writing them," I said. "I'm just trying to confirm information that I heard, in case it's helpful. Clearly, there were some people who didn't like Annabelle, and someone who was making threats might have been willing to carry them out."

"The police said she died of natural causes," Kenzie retorted. "You're acting like she was murdered."

There was a scraping noise behind me. I turned and looked at the objects on the fireplace mantel. *Has that vase always been in that spot?* Damien, again, wasn't looking at me, and I wished I was a mind-reader rather than a conjuror. I really wanted to know what was going on in his head.

"Yes, Annabelle was getting threats. And, if it was murder," Omar said grimly, "then it was someone who clearly knew what they were doing."

Or, it was just someone who knew how to kill a fairy. I really wanted to ask Omar if he knew about the supernatural world, but if his answer was *no*, then things would get uncomfortable really quickly. Unless he dropped some hint, I had to keep guarding the secret of the Sanctuary from him.

Winston put a hand on Kenzie's shoulder. She was staring intently at a spot on the carpet, and her hands were curled into fists. "I think," he said gently, "we should move on from this subject. The police have given their findings, and there's no need to go throwing accusations around."

I wanted to reiterate that I wasn't accusing Kenzie of anything, but Winston was right. By that point, I felt like I was talking in circles, and until we had some new information, there was no reason to keep speculating.

Omar sniffed loudly and reached out to brace himself on the bookcase. "She was my world. What am I going to do without her?"

"I live at Cowboy's Corral," I said. "You probably didn't notice, but I was sitting in the lobby when you checked in on Friday. If you need to talk, you're welcome to stop by my apartment."

Omar's head snapped up, and his expression was everything I had been hoping for. I had called him out on his story about not arriving in Nightmare until Saturday, and he knew there was no lying his way out of it.

"I didn't want to drag his name into this," Omar said carefully, "but there's a guy in this town who's obsessed with Annabelle. He sends her flowers every week, even though she told him a hundred times that she had started dating me. I think the only thing that kept him from showing up at her apartment in Denver was the idea of me going after him."

"We know Hal had an unhealthy interest in Annabelle," I said. "What does that have to do with you and I staying at the same motel?"

"I wanted to come here with Annabelle, so I could keep her safe from that guy, but she said she was a big girl who could take care of herself. I didn't feel as confident about it as she did, so I followed her here. I was going to tell her, eventually, but first I wanted to find Hal and have a little chat with him. Of course, after I got here, I found out I was too late to keep Annabelle safe."

Omar coming to Nightmare to make sure Hal kept his distance sounded plausible. People's feelings for Annabelle seemed to be intense, whether they loved her or hated her, and I had to assume Omar's love of Annabelle was just as strong as Hal's. He was the jealous boyfriend who wanted her all to himself. But could he have killed her?

"I just want to get all the details I can, then go back home to Denver," Omar continued. His shoulders slumped. "Though it doesn't really matter where I go, because she won't be there with me. My life will never be as good now that she's gone."

Kenzie spoke up unexpectedly. "You'll be okay, in time. At least she didn't leave you for someone else."

I wanted to argue that death was a lot worse—and a lot more final—than a breakup, but I had already put Kenzie on her guard by bringing up the threats, and there was no reason to get her more worked up.

Winston stood and reached out to shake Omar's hand. "Again, we are so sorry for your loss. If you need me for anything, you know where to find me."

"Thanks, but the sooner I get out of this awful town, the better."

Damien and I walked Winston, Kenzie, and Omar out the front door of the building. As the three of them moved toward their cars, still talking together, I said to Damien, "That was close! What was upsetting you so much?"

Damien looked at me like I was speaking a foreign language. "What are you talking about? I'm not upset."

"You must be. Otherwise, you wouldn't have moved the photo and the vase with your mind. Was it Winston who made your emotions spike?"

Damien shook his head. "If things were moving inside my office, then it wasn't me doing it."

"Then, who…?"

CHAPTER TWENTY-SIX

"It must have been one of our visitors," Damien said.

"Which means one of them is supernatural, and they probably knew Annabelle was a fairy. They knew exactly how to kill her, and how to make it look natural in the eyes of the police." My chest felt tight as I watched Omar and Winston smile at each other and shake hands again.

"Kenzie had the best motive," Damien pointed out.

"And she got really defensive when I brought up the threatening notes Annabelle was receiving. If we hurry, we can stop them before they leave." Without waiting for Damien to respond, I began to sprint toward the parking area.

"Conjure a delay!" Damien commanded. He fell into step next to me as I focused on how much I wanted our guests to stay exactly where they were. Despite my focus, I watched as Winston opened the door of his car and slid into the driver's seat while Kenzie opened the passenger-side door.

And then, as Damien and I got closer to the cars, Winston got back out, lifted the hood, and peered at the engine. I stopped, laughing and gasping for breath all at once. Had my conjuring been successful, or was it a huge coincidence that Winston's car wasn't working? It didn't matter. Damien and I had gotten what we wanted.

Damien patted me on the back. "Great work," he whispered. Unlike me, he wasn't winded at all.

Omar joined Winston under the hood. "It sounded like a dead battery."

"A psychic would have seen that coming," I said pointedly. At the moment, I didn't much care whether Omar knew about the supernatural world or not.

Winston and Omar turned as one to look at me, and Omar frowned slightly. "A psychic?" he repeated.

Damien seemed to catch on to my comment. "Actually," he said, "not all psychics can see the future. Of course, not all of them can move objects with their mind, either."

Kenzie banged on the roof of Winston's car. "Let's go!"

"We can't," Winston said. "Not until we get a jump."

"But I just want to go home!" Kenzie gulped in a breath and started to cry.

"You and me, both," Omar mumbled. "But I've got cables. I can get your battery going."

Winston came around the side of the car and slid an arm around Kenzie's shoulders. "It's okay. Omar will give us a jump, then we'll drive straight back to the farm."

"Why are you so anxious to leave, Kenzie?" I asked. I was trying really hard not to sound accusatory.

Kenzie glared at me. "The woman my boyfriend left me for died right where I work, and I had to watch him make a fool of himself while this whole stupid town brought flowers and lit candles for her like she was some kind of a saint. Now I have to stand here and listen to you weirdos talk about psychics. I'm done. I'm just done with the whole thing."

"They're not weirdos," Winston reprimanded. "We've had a good relationship with the Sanctuary for years."

"I don't know what's good about it. They come once a year and make money on your property, then go back to living their strange lives in this rat hole." Kenzie turned her eyes to Damien. "What have you ever done for us, except bring that awful girl here to get in the way of my relationship with Hal?"

"Kenzie!" Winston shrank back, his arm sliding away from Kenzie's shoulders. He sounded more sad than angry. "How can you say those things? No one here meant to hurt you, and you know that."

Winston had sounded so gleeful in the wake of Annabelle's murder, since he had been picturing all the people who would flock to the festival to see the scene of the crime. He probably hadn't stopped to think how all that focus on Annabelle would make his own assistant manager feel. She had to stand by and watch as the woman she hated was remembered as a beautiful soul who was taken too soon.

"Winston is right," I told Kenzie. "None of us here knew about Annabelle's relationship with Hal. You knew all about it, though, and you were the one who sent her the threatening notes, weren't you?"

"So what if I was?" Kenzie spat. "I didn't murder her, like you seem to think."

Suddenly, I thought of the jack-o'-lantern Kenzie had nearly tripped over at the festival. Maybe her mind was like Damien's. As heightened as her emotions were, she could have telekinetically pulled that pumpkin to herself without realizing it. Maybe she had been the one moving objects in Damien's office.

"Again, no one is accusing you of murder," Damien said.

A tear slid down Kenzie's cheek, and the anger seemed to drain out of her. "I didn't want her to come back here. Even though I'd lost Hal, I knew I wouldn't be able to bear seeing the two of them together. Hal knew her address, because he sent her flowers all the time. He never did that for me. I went to his place and said I wanted to figure out how we could be friends again, and when he left the room to get us drinks, I went through his phone to find her address."

"You hoped threatening Annabelle would keep her from coming back here," I said, "but it didn't work."

"I can't believe she showed up again! I even had to talk to your group before the party, and she just smirked at me the whole time. The only thing that made it hurt less was seeing the way she brushed off Hal that night. I knew right away I wouldn't have to see the two of them together again, because she was over it."

"I'm sorry, Kenzie," Winston said sadly. "Annabelle was so good at getting people to spend money, and all I could think of was how much she would help us have a record year if she was working at the festival again. I never considered how it would make you feel."

Ah-ha! I had been right. When it came to Annabelle, Winston had only seen dollar signs, so much so that he had even tried to hire her full-time. It hadn't been about her ethereal glow at all.

I was surprised to feel a sudden wave of sympathy for Kenzie. It hadn't been right for her to threaten Annabelle, but I did feel sorry for the way neither Hal nor Winston had considered her feelings. Both of them had acted selfishly, albeit in two completely different ways.

Just as I thought that, I saw movement out of the corner of my eye. It was Malcolm, coming around the side of the building, a small black umbrella shading his face from the sun. *I guess we've all done things we're not proud of.*

"What do you want from us?" Omar asked suddenly. He had been standing to one side silently, watching our exchange, and he crossed his arms in front of his chest. "You ran out here for what? Just to ask more questions and to make bizarre comments about psychics? I thought we agreed the police were correct. Annabelle died of natural causes, and I would like to go home and mourn my girl-friend in peace."

"Then go," Damien said. "No one is stopping you."

Omar hesitated. He was acting as if Annabelle's death had been explained, but he seemed to agree with Damien and me that there was more to the story. "I said I'd give them a jump. Plus, what about her paycheck?" he asked, clearly looking for an excuse not to leave. "The money will go toward her funeral. And you, Winston. I'll need the money from you, too."

Winston laughed sardonically. "She didn't work for me again this year, remember? She yelled at me and called me names, instead, all because I had offered her a full-time job."

"You did what?" Kenzie shouted, rounding on Winston.

The hood of Winston's car slammed shut, and all of us jumped. Omar, who was closest to the car, let out a yelp of surprise. The picture frame, the vase, and the car hood had all moved, seemingly on their own, since our visitors had arrived. But whose mind had moved them?

"She was my moneymaker," Winston said. "I've already apologized for not stopping to consider your feel-ings, Kenzie, but Annabelle turned me down, anyway. She was so mad that I asked her to quit Nightmare Sanctuary that she wouldn't even come work for me part-time again."

Malcolm had walked up to us, and he wordlessly leaned in and sniffed.

"Do we smell bad?" Winston asked, eyeing Malcolm.

"I detect just a whiff of death." Malcolm met my gaze, his eyes glittering. He continued to sniff loudly as Omar, Winston, and Kenzie all took a step back from him.

"Kenzie was right," Winston said. "What a creepy bunch of people you are. I can't believe Annabelle would rather work here than out at the festival with us normal folks. She could have made so much money. Instead, she humiliated me in front of all those people."

And, afterward, I dumped ticket stubs all over the floor, because the bin wasn't in its proper spot. It had been moved, but not intentionally.

"She could have made so much money for herself, or for you?" I asked as everything clicked. "I've been so focused on Annabelle's romantic entanglements and Daniel's resentment of her that I've overlooked what this was really about. Winston, you've mentioned before that the money from the festival keeps your farm afloat. Annabelle was good at getting people to shell out their cash, and you needed her to do the same thing for you again this year. When she turned you down, you snapped."

"What a stupid theory." Winston was glaring at me.

"When we were talking in Damien's office earlier," I continued, "you didn't look nervous when we discussed the murder angle, but your actions spoke louder than your words, didn't they? But all those things in Damien's office weren't the first things you've moved recently. Before that, it was the ticket bin the night Annabelle yelled at you and the jack-o'-lantern Kenzie stepped on at the festival."

Winston's lips pulled back, his teeth bared. "I never wanted to be like you people! I didn't want to be a freak. So I took over my parents' farm, and I lived a normal life, and I struggled to make ends meet. Things have been hard the past couple of years, and I knew if I didn't make a killing on the festival this year, I might lose the farm."

"So when Annabelle turned down your job offer, you thought it was the end of your farm," I said. "Did you kill her out of frustration, or because you thought her death was the only way for you to make a buck off of her?"

Winston didn't answer. Instead, he turned and ran, heading for the dirt road. Malcolm dropped his umbrella and took off after him, a blur of movement. He really was a predator who was honed to hunt down a human. In seconds, Malcolm had tackled Winston to the ground.

The rest of us ran over as Winston began to shout. "No one should have ever known! Any normal human would have thought it was natural causes! I didn't think you freaks would be so nosy!"

I put my hands on my hips and stuck out my chest proudly. "Olivia Kendrick, Nosy Freak. I like the sound of that."

Omar looked both confused and angry. "Freaks? How dare you talk about my girlfriend and her co-workers like that! She was unusual, sure, but she was special."

So Omar didn't know he had been dating a fairy. I looked at Damien, and we exchanged little nods. We had been right not to speak openly about the supernatural in front of the group. Our mention of psychics had gotten Omar's attention, but we hadn't crossed the line.

"There's one thing I don't understand," I said. "Annabelle was giggling right before she died, like she was with somebody she liked, but she was so angry at you, Winston. How did you get her to trust you again?"

"I played to her ego, of course," Winston said sourly. "I apologized and told her she was the most popular employee I'd ever had, because she was so beautiful and charismatic. I told her the candy was a peace offering. I know that maze backwards and forwards, and I was probably out of it before she took her last breath. I even took paths that didn't take me past any of you so I wouldn't be seen. I should have never gotten caught."

"I'm calling the police," Damien said as he pulled out his phone. "Olivia, go get Zach and ask him to come help keep an eye on Winston."

I ran inside the Sanctuary and found Zach in the ticket office. He eagerly joined us out front, looking excited at the prospect of holding down a murderer, but it was clear Malcolm had the situation under control. Winston was lying limp on the ground, moaning now and then.

Malcolm was crouched over Winston, and I leaned closer to hear what he was saying. "You killed her by covering her mouth and nose, just like you did to make her swallow the candy. You suffocated her." He was coaching Winston how to confess to Annabelle's murder without involving anything supernatural.

Winston was still moaning when the police arrived, and I wasn't surprised to see that Officer Reyes was one of them. After he had put Winston in handcuffs and loaded him into the back of the patrol car, Reyes shook my hand. "At the rate you're going," he said, "we're going to have to put you on the payroll."

CHAPTER TWENTY-SEVEN

"I didn't actually smell death, you know," Malcolm said.

We were standing in the dining room, waiting for the family meeting to begin. It had been just over twenty-four hours since Winston's arrest. After he had been hauled off by the Nightmare Police Department, we'd had to calm down Kenzie and Omar, who were both understandably shaken by Winston's confession. Eventually, though, Kenzie had called her mom for a ride home, and Omar had hit the road back to Denver.

After that, I had wanted nothing more than a nap, but those of us who worked at the Sanctuary had to suck it up and get through a long night of work. I had slept like a rock Sunday night, and my Monday so far had been bliss-fully uneventful. As soon as I had arrived in the dining room, Malcolm had sidled up next to me, a sly look on his face as he told me his sniffing the day before had just been for show.

"If you didn't detect the death stench," I asked Malcolm, "then why did you say you did?"

"I thought it might draw out the killer, if they were present."

"And, of course, they were present. Winston's secret telekinetic ability wound up being the key to solving the murder. His emotions were so heightened during our meeting, he was mentally moving objects in Damien's office. I didn't realize he was behind it, at first, but I knew the killer must have been him, Kenzie, or Omar. Then, when I realized he had been the only one of the three present the night the ticket stub bin got moved, I knew it had to be Winston. He had seemed so calm on the outside, sometimes wildly happy, even, but inside, he was terrified of losing his farm. Annabelle's refusal to work for him made him so angry he killed her out of spite."

Malcolm tapped his index finger against his jaw. "And because he had some tie to the supernatural world, he recognized Annabelle as a fairy, which meant he knew she wouldn't be able to resist the honey candy."

I nodded. "Remember Ross Banning, the reporter from *The Nightmare Journal*? He was a secret shapeshifter. Then there's Winston, who's also got supernatural abilities but was pretending to be normal. How many more of Nightmare's residents are hiding secrets like that?"

"Every town has its secrets," Malcolm said. "Nightmare is no exception."

"I suppose. It's funny, I had been so focused on love being the motive for Annabelle's murder that I almost missed the money angle. Again, though, Winston's mind tricks made me consider other options." I sighed. "I feel kind of bad for the guy, or at least I would, if he wasn't a killer. I know what it's like when a lack of money makes you feel desperate."

"Indeed. Your financial desperation is how you wound up here with us freaks, after all." Malcolm put a hand on my shoulder. "Thank you for accepting me as I am, dark past and all."

I leaned in and hugged Malcolm. As I was straightening up, I heard Lucy's voice rise above the din in the room. "Silly dog! Don't do that!" I looked over to see

Felipe gnawing on her pink sneaker. Lucy was laughing and making shooing motions at Felipe.

"I'd better go help out with the *dog*," I told Malcolm, emphasizing the last word. Lucy had finally realized she could see ghosts, but she didn't yet know about the rest of the supernatural world. We'd wait a bit before breaking the news to her that Felipe was a chupacabra.

Mori called to Felipe as I walked up to the group, and he immediately let go of Lucy's shoe, which was covered in drool. Lucy clutched at her throat and made a gagging sound. "Gross!" she yelled, even though she was grinning.

Damien was sitting nearby, and he laughed. "We said we'd take you through the haunt once it opens for the night, but maybe you should be one of the people doing the haunting. You have a flair for the dramatic."

Lucy stopped gagging and started jumping up and down. "You mean I can be one of the scary people?"

"If you want."

"Yes!" Lucy pumped her fist, then spread her arms wide, fingers splayed. "I'm going to be in the haunt!"

"I'll go make the arrangements," Damien said. He gave me a wink as he stood and headed toward the front of the room. That afternoon, he had made good on his promise to give Lucy a behind-the-scenes tour of the Sanctuary. Of course, I had come along since I knew how much fun it would be. Lucy had loved the Sanctuary the one time she had been through it, and she had been even more excited to learn all of its secrets and see the effects up close with the lights on.

Felipe settled down enough that Lucy was able to pet him, and watching their interaction occupied my time until Justine started the family meeting. As soon as she stepped up to the podium, Lucy sat down on a bench, folded her hands on the table, and listened attentively. She was taking being a Sanctuary "employee" very seriously.

When it was time to dole out assignments, Justine said, "Olivia, you'll be in the lagoon vignette tonight. Also, we have a very special guest employee tonight: Miss Lucy Dalton." Justine gestured toward our table as Lucy waved grandly. There was a round of applause for her, as well as a few shouts and cheers. When everyone quieted down again, Justine told Lucy she would be a pirate alongside me.

When the family meeting wrapped up, I took Lucy to the costume room. Damien had already made plans for her, and a white pirate shirt was waiting, complete with full sleeves and lacy cuffs. It was way too big to fit Lucy as a shirt, but with a black leather belt, it made a perfect pirate dress. Lucy could wear it with her black leggings, but that still left her with pink light-up sneakers.

Damien came in as we were wondering what to do about shoes. He held up his hand, a small pair of black lace-up boots clutched in his fingers. "Maida had an extra pair. Since she and Lucy are about the same size, they should fit perfectly."

Mori had come along with us, and she offered to give Lucy what she called a pirate makeover. The two of them moved to one of the makeup tables, leaving me alone with Damien for the first time since I had arrived at the Sanctuary with Lucy.

"I spent most of the day practicing," he said, almost casually.

"That's great!"

"Well, after you conjured a dead battery on Winston's car, I knew I had to start working on my own abilities if I'm ever going to catch up."

I waved a hand as if it were no big deal, even though I was beaming with pride. "It could have been a coincidence. But back to you and your training. How many things did you break today?"

"None!" Damien laughed. "Of course, that's because I practiced in the middle of nowhere. I did uproot one sapling, and a raven flew right into my face. I'm pretty sure it wasn't aiming for me. Instead, I pulled it toward me."

"Ouch. Was the raven okay?"

"Don't you want to know if I'm okay?" Damien drew his eyebrows together in an effort to look insulted.

"Your face looks like it always does, so you clearly survived."

"Yeah. The bird did, too. It yelled at me a bit, then flew off."

I chuckled at the idea of Damien getting an earful from a raven, but he didn't seem to share my mirth. Instead, he looked hesitant, so I prompted, "Did something else happen?"

"I think I heard my mother's voice. It was really distant, like the wind was carrying it from somewhere far away, but it told me to keep going."

"She's encouraging you," I said. I reached out and took Damien's hand, giving it a squeeze. "She's proud of you, and so am I."

"I still have a long way to go."

"So do I, but we'll get there together."

Lucy ran up to us right then. "How do I look?" She struck what I think was supposed to be a fearsome pose.

"You look like the most terrifying child pirate who ever sailed!" I said.

"I think you're going to make dozens of people scream tonight." Damien grinned at Lucy.

"Let me get into my costume, then we'll head to the lagoon vignette," I said. It was only as I stepped toward the rack of costumes that I realized I was still holding Damien's hand. Feeling a flush of embarrassment, I let go, found my costume, and hustled into a changing room. By the time I emerged in my pirate costume, my cheeks had returned to their usual color. Just in case I had another embarrassing moment, though, I put on extra blush at the makeup table, so my cheeks would be rosy no matter what.

"Remember," I told Lucy as we headed out of the costume room, "you need to be changed out of your costume and ready to go by nine thirty. That's when your dad is picking you up since it's a school night."

"Who needs school when I can be a pirate?" Lucy bounded down the hallway, flapping her arms so the sleeves billowed out. "Let's go scare people!"

There was a loud whistle, and suddenly, Tanner and McCrory appeared beside Lucy. "Lead on, little lady!" Tanner shouted.

Lucy stopped, looking from one ghost to the other with her mouth open. I hurried to catch up to her, worried she would be scared by their sudden appearance. Instead, her face lit up as she turned to me. "This is going to be the best Halloween ever!"

A NOTE FROM THE AUTHOR

I'll let you in on a little secret: Malcolm is one of my favorite Nightmare residents. I was so happy to share his backstory in this book. I hope you're enjoying getting to know these characters better, too.

Thank you for reading *Poisoning at the Party* and for still being here, five books into the series! There's a lot more fun in store for Olivia and her friends, but before you head on to the next book, will you please leave a review for this one? Those reviews really make a difference, and I'm grateful for every one.

Eternally Yours,

Beth

P.S. You can keep up with my latest book news, get fun freebies, and more by signing up for my newsletter at BethDolgner.com!

Clawing at the Corral

NIGHTMARE, ARIZONA BOOK SIX
PARANORMAL COZY MYSTERIES

Horses, Homicide, and Hope in Nightmare, Arizona

Olivia Kendrick has déjà vu. The star of Nightmare's popular Wild West Stunt Show is found dead after a heated argument, and it looks like an animal attack. Olivia knows better, though. The scene is eerily similar to the first murder she ever investigated in Nightmare.

There's a young new stunt rider eager to take over the starring role, but he's not the only one with a motive for murder. As clues mount about money problems, old grudges, and unbridled ambition, the suspect list only gets longer.

To make things worse, someone from Olivia's past unexpectedly shows up in Nightmare, and he's one of the suspects. The newcomer throws Olivia's boss, Damien Shackleford, into a psychic crisis. Can Olivia help him control his power before someone gets hurt?

ACKNOWLEDGMENTS

Alex, David, Kristine, Lisa, Mom, and Sabrina: thank you for being the most eagle-eyed test readers ever. You catch my little typos and my giant plot holes alike. Many thanks to Lia at Your Best Book Editor and Trish at Blossoming Pages for your editing skills and patience. Jena at Book-Mojo, thank you for putting my stories into such a gorgeous package! And, of course, thank you to my team of ARC readers for your enthusiasm and support.

ABOUT THE AUTHOR

Beth Dolgner writes paranormal fiction and nonfiction. Her interest in things that go bump in the night really took off on a trip to Savannah, Georgia, so it's fitting that her first series—Betty Boo, Ghost Hunter—takes place in that spooky city. Beth also writes paranormal nonfiction, including her first book, *Georgia Spirits and Specters*, which is a collection of Georgia ghost stories.

Beth and her husband, Ed, live in Tucson, Arizona. Their Victorian bungalow is possibly haunted, but it's not nearly as exciting as the ghostly activity at Eternal Rest Bed and Breakfast.

Beth also enjoys giving presentations on Victorian death and mourning traditions as well as Victorian Spiritualism. She has been a volunteer at an historic cemetery, a ghost tour guide, and a paranormal investigator. Beth likes to think of it all as research for her books.

Keep up with Beth and sign up for her newsletter at BethDolgner.com.

BOOKS BY BETH DOLGNER

The Nightmare, Arizona Series

Paranormal Cozy Mystery

Homicide at the Haunted House

Drowning at the Diner

Slaying at the Saloon

Murder at the Motel

Poisoning at the Party

Clawing at the Corral (June 2024)

The Eternal Rest Bed and Breakfast Series

Paranormal Cozy Mystery

Sweet Dreams

Late Checkout

Picture Perfect

Scenic Views

Breakfast Included

Groups Welcome

Quiet Nights

The Betty Boo, Ghost Hunter Series

Romantic Urban Fantasy

Ghost of a Threat

Ghost of a Whisper

Ghost of a Memory

Ghost of a Hope

Manifest

Young Adult Steampunk

A Talent for Death

Young Adult Urban Fantasy

Nonfiction

Georgia Spirits and Specters

Everyday Voodoo